ADVANCE PRAISE FOR
THE WAYANG AT EIGHT

GW01066292

"I am glad that Gregory Nalpon's work at last has a chance of being recognised. His stories are excellent."

—**Edwin Thumboo,** award-winning Singaporean poet and academic

"Gregory Nalpon wrote from the margins about a Singapore in the throes of great change, and I am convinced that he is our first true proponent of magical realism."

—**Robert Yeo**, author of *The Adventures of Holden Heng*

"Gregory Nalpon's stories and evocative commentaries might seem nostalgic for a pre-development Singapore, but make no mistake—there is little sentimentality here, as marginalised characters get fleshed out with brutality, as well as compassion. His poetic, fable-esque narratives possess a sense of magic that is almost spiritual, full of moral lessons about the abjection of human desires, death, and a knowing presence at the heart of the natural world."

—**Cyril Wong**, author of *Unmarked Treasure*
    and *The Last Lesson of Mrs de Souza*

"Gregory Nalpon's stories are perfectly poised between gritty realism and mythic wonder. He observes and embraces the rich local diversity of Singapore with the eye of an enchanted poet and the heart of an honest friend. He fathoms the human soul through, and beyond, cultural identity. Editor Angus Whitehead's love for Nalpon glows in this informative and accessible edition, which will be a treasure for Singaporeans, and a gratifying find for the rest of us who are eager for great reads from around the globe, or take interest in the development of post-colonial writing. Nalpon deserves to claim a place among the most unique and significant voices of the formative and vibrant 1970s."

—**Tristanne Connolly**, Associate Professor of English,
    St. Jerome's University

THE WAYANG AT EIGHT MILESTONE

Stories & Essays

GREGORY NALPON

Edited by Angus Whitehead

EPIGRAM BOOKS / SINGAPORE

Published in Singapore by Epigram Books
www.epigrambooks.sg

Cover design and layout by Andrew Lee

These pieces were originally published in the following places:
"The Rose and the Silver Key," *Singapore Short Stories* (2 vols.), ed. by Robert Yeo, 1978; "A Soul For Anna Lim," *Her World*, April 1976; "A Knocking on the Door," *Her World*, October 1975; "The Appointment," *Her World*, December 1975; "The Hunter Lays Down His Spear", newspaper column, further details unknown, c. 1975; "A Man Without Song," *The Straits Times*, 3 August 1975; "Lion City Filled with Panthers", newspaper column, further details unknown, c. 1975; "My Say," *Her World*, September 1975

Published with the support of

NATIONAL ARTS COUNCIL
SINGAPORE

National Library Board, Singapore Cataloguing-in-Publication Data

Nalpon, Gregory (1938-1978)
The wayang at eight milestone: stories & essays / Gregory Nalpon ; edited by Angus Whitehead. –
Singapore : Epigram Books, 2013.
p. cm

ISBN: 978-981-07-6457-9 (paperback)
ISBN: 978-981-07-6458-6 (ebook)

1. Singapore – Social life and customs –20th century.
2. Singapore – Fiction. I. Whitehead, Angus. II. Title.

PR9570.S53
S828 -- dc23 OCN855728813
First Edition: October 2013
10 9 8 7 6 5 4 3 2 1

FOR MONA

CONTENTS

PREFACE

IT GIVES US great pleasure to see—finally!—a collection of our father's short stories and other writings published in Singapore. Papa always protested that his pieces were "not good enough for anyone to read" and that "more corrections needed to be made". We beg to differ, as we did then, almost forty years ago: a collection of Gregory Stanislaus Nalpon's stories of *his* Singapore is long overdue.

For over three decades, manuscripts of Papa's stories in his unique hand have lain undisturbed in a red suitcase in Singapore, others carefully kept in Papworth Everard, in Cambridgeshire, England. It has been a joy for us to rediscover and transcribe them in places Papa would have loved: on beaches, in pubs and quiet rooms in France and England.

We very much hope you enjoy—as we have—encountering these miniatures, Gregory Nalpon's attempts to capture a slightly earlier, but now very much lost, Singapore.

Jacinta & Zero Nalpon
May 2013

INTRODUCTION

DURING MY FIRST YEAR working in Singapore (2008) I faced a long journey home: an hour or more on a nondescript MRT train from Boon Lay back east to Bedok. One book I recall whiling away those journeys with was a tatty Heinemann Asia copy of *Singapore Short Stories* picked up at an NIE book sale. Wedged between largely silent fellow travellers, I first encountered Stella Kon's knowing "The Martyrdom of Helena Rodriguez", three sardonic-ambivalent strokes of Arthur Yap's genius, and Catherine Lim's tell-tale proto/faux-Singlish "The Taximan's Story" (perhaps even more pertinent thirty years on). But the story that intrigued me most was Gregory Nalpon's local-quotidian fairy tale (or national allegory?) "The Rose and the Silver Key".

I was eager to read more. At the end of the book I found a brief biographical notice: "The late Gregory Nalpon [...] has numerous other stories which await collection and publication."[1] So there were more stories? Where were they now? And who exactly was the "late Gregory Nalpon"?

Upon its original publication in 1978, Malcolm M. Mercer, in his review of *Singapore Short Stories*, declared that, "[p]oignancy is [...] reflected in 'The Rose and the Silver Key' by Gregory Nalpon [...] to my mind one of the most stimulating of all the [twelve] authors in this collection".[2] During the early-mid 1990s, *Singapore Short Stories* was one of the first local texts to be studied for O-Level Literature in English examinations in Singapore. Thus, hundreds of young Singaporeans, now in their mid-thirties, must have read, written about, or even seen performed, "The Rose and the Silver Key",[3] yet almost two decades on, no one I spoke to seemed to have heard of Gregory Nalpon. While I did discover Nalpon's lighter, nostalgic "A Girl as Sweet as Alice" (reprinted here in its original form as "The Courtship of Donatello Varga") in another short story anthology, I eventually abandoned hope of locating the unpublished stories.

However, one afternoon in September 2011, while absent-mindedly searching online, I came across a third Nalpon story, the John Steinbeck-influenced, ingeniously local-satiric "A Man without Song", published in *The Straits Times* in 1975. The same site revealed details of Nalpon's careers as court advocate for the Singapore Manual and Mercantile Workers Union, and as a radio and newspaper journalist. While a writer since his schooldays at Saint Joseph's Institution, it seems that Nalpon, a perfectionist never completely satisfied with his own work, must have only seriously considered publishing his stories around 1975, three years before his untimely death at just 40 years old.

Gregory Nalpon's funeral notice in *The Straits Times* helped me to locate and contact his son, Zero Nalpon. Mr Nalpon, now an eminent lawyer in Singapore, kindly put me in touch with his elder sister Jacinta, a nurse working in the UK. As luck would have it, Ms Nalpon was about to travel to Singapore, and yes, she and her brother would be happy to talk about their father. Meeting at Mr Nalpon's distinctively furnished shophouse office on Kampung Bahru Road near Outram Park, I also first read the peculiarly wonderful "The Knocking on the Door" and "A Soul For Anna Lim", two of the three stories Nalpon published in *Her World* (1975-6) as well as three published articles, and, fascinatingly, a 1969 birthday present for his close friend, and renowned sports coach, Patrick Zehnder—typewritten passages from Nalpon's favourite authors, John Steinbeck and the Mexican novelist José Rubén Romero. In the weeks that followed, Jacinta, on her return to the UK, sent me, along with fascinating anecdotes about her father, three of his unpublished stories: "The Mango Tree", "An Eye for an Eye" and "Mei-Lin". These stories were as good as, if not better than, the published ones.

The following spring when visiting Singapore, Jacinta happily surprised me again by reading aloud, in the rain on Bras Basah Road, the short but evocative and angry "The Old Woman of Bukit Ho Swee". So there were indeed numerous Nalpon stories awaiting collection. Why had they not been collected and published before? During his lifetime, Nalpon appears to have been reluctant to publish many of his stories, and a subsequent attempt to publish the short stories in the 1990s was abandoned. Thus sole, fragile original manuscript copies of Nalpon's stories, radio plays and other pieces had remained precariously concealed in boxes in Papworth Everard in Cambridgeshire (Jacinta's home) and Singapore. This volume thus finally recovers, collects and preserves for future readers a representative selection of Gregory Nalpon's writing.

For those who encountered him either in life or through his writings, Nalpon must have seemed both unique and eccentric. Few local writers in Singapore in the 1970s can have resembled the tattooed, completely toothless,[4] scooter-riding ex-trade unionist and peripatetic DJ, journalist and dogged habitué of the Singaporean 'ulu'.[5] Nalpon, with his eclectic taste for nature, life on the street as well as high culture, resembled his beloved Ernest Hemingway, or literary heroes such as Steinbeck's Doc in *Cannery Row*, Dumas' Cyrano, Romero's Pito. Indeed Nalpon's stories seem to have grown out of a peculiarly Singaporean life. Even a story as seemingly slight as "The Appointment", a Christmas ghost story in a local women's magazine, apparently emerged out of "The breeze and I are whispering goodbye to dreams we used to share"—lyrics to a record regularly played at the Nalpon home in Jalan Soo Bee: Caterina Valente's "The Breeze and I", in Al Stillman's adaptation of Ernesto Lecuona's *Andalusian Suite*, music beloved of the couple in the story.[6] Quietly unconventional, a nomad on a tiny island, socially engaged and concerned—Nalpon's consistent willingness to help, notably in his legal representation of the poor and disenfranchised, seems to continue into many of his stories.[7]

Patrick Zehnder remembers Nalpon's penchant for the kinds of coffee shops and bars we encounter in "A Soul for Anna Lim", "A Girl as Sweet as Alice", "Mei-Lin", and of course "The Rose and the

Silver Key". In such crowded, socially-local environments, Nalpon, never without a book, would read and write down ideas for stories, plays and essays on the backs of cigarette packets or anything he could lay his hands on.[8] One wonders: was "The Rose and the Silver Key" first conceived in such an environment?

Nalpon was something of a natural storyteller. Collectively the stories comprise a valuable picture of an urban and rural Singapore, of pig breeders, interminable bus rides and only occasional saloon cars, gangsters, sarabat stalls, samshu shops (how many Singaporeans today know what a samshu shop is?), bar girls, wayang, attap huts, seaside coffee shops on stilts, fortune tellers, freshwater wells, hunters, rubber trees and bee hoon factories. In short, a Singapore that was, as Nalpon was all too aware, fast disappearing.

Such a fondness for his pre-developed Singapore, an organically local-multicultural milieu barely imaginable today, was surely coloured by his upbringing (a mother, two sisters and a Chinese step-brother) and continued life at the Nalpon family house at Jalan Soo Bee (the mixture of Malay and Chinese here seems prescient) near the sea at Changi. At the same time, these stories, often conspicuously short, with a slight hint of melodrama, gesture to publication in popular local magazines such as *Her World*. Nalpon was writing for needed money in a young, small country. Conversely, "Mei-Lin" appears to draw on Nalpon's journalistic career and his travels during the late 1950s / early 1960s through Siam, Borneo and Malaya.

In the background of many of these stories, notably "A Man Without Song" and "The Old Woman of Bukit Ho Swee", a careful reader can detect the dreaded *kempetai* headquarters of the Japanese occupation, participants in and witnesses of the Malayan 'emergency', the Maria Hertogh, Hock Lee bus and 1964 and 1969 race riots, the withdrawal of the British, the controversial Bukit Ho Swee fire. Yet it seems significant that Gregory Nalpon, dying in 1978, did not live to witness Lee Kuan Yew's introduction of the national 'Speak Mandarin' campaign. Nalpon's refreshingly unique cross-cultural lens in his stories suggests an alternative kind of nation-building, described by Shirley Lim as a "provisional, unsettled, improvising identity-formation"[9], celebrating the national via democratised, undemonstrative local and mutual appreciations of otherness. Like Lloyd Fernando and Goh Poh Seng, albeit in a wholly different way, Nalpon "contribut[es] to a counter-tradition, resisting the sometimes unsubtle official encouragement of literature that supports and celebrates nation-building projects".[10] Few other Singaporean writers of the 1970s so successfully and consistently represented a local ethno-religious culture neighbouring but not his or her own, while continually, ambiguously crossing cultures.

Nalpon, a descendant of French-speaking South Indian Catholics, was occasionally mistaken as Eurasian. He playfully deploys a similar cultural ambiguity in his stories' representations of characters like Fatimah, Alice, Greenwater Boy, and Masood and his family. In his representations of the black dog spirit penned by nails up a mango tree that supports Awang, Minah and Ruqayya's house in "The Mango Tree", the apparently insane Ruqayya's erotic affection for the tree, Fatimah's apparel, and even the description of the rose in "The Rose and the Silver Key", we encounter a rich fusion of Malay, Indian, Chinese, Western and other cultures through Nalpon's unique, eclectically-fed imagination. The bright beauty of the world of these stories is often suddenly shot through with death, and disturbing human and/or supernatural violence, for which the haunting voice of one of Nalpon's favourite singers, Yma Sumac, would make an ideal soundtrack. Significantly, much of the action in his stories occurs in lamp-lit night. Might then we call, for instance, "The Mango Tree", "An Eye for an Eye", "A Soul for Anna Lim" or even "A Knocking at the Door" examples of an early post-colonial Singapore gothic?

In these stories, the magical/miraculous seem very much a reality. One thinks in this context of Nalpon's daughter, Jacinta, named after a Portuguese 'saint', one of three children who encountered and communed with the Virgin Mary at Fatima in the final years of the first world war.

Nalpon, eccentric, freethinking rather than subversive, ahead of his time in his local cosmopolitanism, a media-hungry citizen of the world who never physically travelled farther than Siam and Malaya (as was), seems a local idiosyncrasy: an Indian Singaporean writer seemingly largely unfettered by the standpoints of nation and culture. Yet such imaginative and socially conscious writing in the increasingly authoritarian Singapore of the 1970s was not without personal cost. For Nalpon's sister Bridget, "in his writings, Gregory represented the unheard voice of the Singapore people and their culture. I think he was misunderstood, ignored and often lonely."[11] Too little known during his lifetime and neglected after his death, for me Gregory Nalpon seems one of Singapore's most exciting and genuinely inventive early writers. It is hoped that through this collection, Nalpon's accessible, memorable and gratifyingly ambiguous stories should finally obtain the readership they deserve.

—

My thanks to Patrick Zehnder; Bridget Egbuna; the staff at Epigram Books, especially editor Jason Erik Lundberg and publisher Edmund Wee for their enthusiastic support of this project. I would also like to thank Aliah Ali, Jagit Kaur Major Singh and Chong Yin Fong at Singapore Press Holdings; Connie Chng and Hua Hong Koon at Pearson Longman, Angelia Poon and Farah Roslan at NIE, and most especially to Mona, Jacinta and Zero Nalpon. Jacinta tirelessly transcribed the majority of these texts from fragile manuscript pages to Word documents that then formed the basis of this edition of Nalpon's writings.

I would also like to express my gratitude to Nithiya, Samantha, Nurul, Nicholyn, Edward, Zhi Wen, Hannah, Debbie, Annie, Ernest, Chin Yee, Matthew, Fabian, Perdana and Su Peng, my fifteen Year 2 BA Literature students taking the "Singapore and the Region in Literature Course" at the National Institute of Education, NTU, Singapore, January 2013 semester. Their positive responses to and perceptive readings of Nalpon's texts futher enhanced my enthusiasm for this project.

Finally I am grateful to Jinat for her patience and support as I obsessively immersed myself in the life and work of this 'unknown' but increasingly fascinating Singaporean writer.

—

In editing this collection of Gregory Nalpon's stories and other writings, I have relied upon either previously published material or transcriptions of increasingly fragile manuscript material currently in the UK and sent to me as digital files by Jacinta Nalpon. Jacinta has also kindly checked my edited manuscript against the original manuscripts. A wealth of manuscript material has yet to be transcribed and it is hoped that further volumes of Gregory Nalpon's writings will be published in the future.

We did our best to ascertain where material had been previously published, and gratefully acknowledge that source for permission to reproduce here. However, we were unsuccessful in the cases of "The Hunter Lays Down his Spear" and "Lion City Filled with Panthers". All other material as far as we know is published for the first time here. However, we would be very grateful if omissions could be communicated to us at whitehead65_99@yahoo.co.uk.

Angus Whitehead
August 2013

[1] *Singapore Short Stories*, 121.

[2] Malcolm M. Mercer, review of Robert Yeo, ed., *Singapore Short Stories* Volumes I & II, Singapore Book World, Volume 9 (Singapore: National Book Development Council of Singapore, 1978), 56.

[3] See "S'pore Short Stories a sell-out", *Straits Times*, 15 June 1991.

[4] As Robert Yeo recalled (conversation with editor, November 2011).

[5] Nalpon's tattoos included the words 'Love' and 'Mona', his wife's name, inscribed on his knuckles (Jacinta Nalpon, conversation with editor, October 2011). He also had a small pet monkey he named Gaugin (Bridget Egbuna, email, 4 November 2012).

[6] Nalpon adored music, books, films and all things South American.

[7] Nalpon's younger sister recalls in the bad floods of 1954 the 16-year-old Gregory Nalpon helping the small Chinese farmers save their pigs from drowning (Bridget Egbuna, email, 4 November 2012).

[8] Goh Poh Seng, the author of arguably the first Singapore novel also "eavesdropped shamelessly" at sarabat stalls, coffee shops and what Koh Tai Ann describes as "seedy bard in less salubrious districts" (xiv). See Koh Tai Ann, "Goh Poh Seng, If We Dream Too Long: An Appreciation'", Goh Poh Seng, *If We Dream Too Long* (Singapore: NTU Press, 2010), xix, n. 21.

[9] Shirley Lim, 'Introduction: 1965-1990', in Angelia Poon, Philip Holden and Shirley Lim, eds., *Writing Singapore: An Historical Anthology of Singapore Literature* (Singapore: NUS Press, 2009), 177.

[10] Lim, 179.

[11] Bridget Egbuna, email, 4 November 2012.

Criticism on Nalpon and

Other Sources Consulted

Anon., "New Floating Dispensary for Islands", *Straits Times*, 19 January 1951, 5.

Anon., "Pulau Pawai Men Say: No Ghosts", *Straits Times*, 20 August 1950, 3.

Anon., "Rape hunt—Police Look for 'Playboy'", *Straits Times*, 29 May 1957, 7.

Frank Brennan, Notes on "Singapore Short Stories" (Singapore: Heinemann Asia, 1991).

Kah Seng Loh, "The 1961 Kampong Bukit Ho Swee fire and the making of modern Singapore", doctoral thesis, Murdoch University, 2009. http://researchrepository.murdoch.edu.au/750/

Shirley Lim, "Introduction, Singapore, 1965-1990", Angelia Poon, Shirley Geok-lin Lim, eds. *Writing Singapore; A Historical Anthology of Singapore Literature* (Singapore: NUS Press, 2009), 173-81.

Malcolm M. Mercer, review of Singapore Short Stories Volumes I & II, *Singapore Book World*, Volume 9 (Singapore: National Book Development Council of Singapore, 1978), 56.

Oxford English Dictionary, online edition.

Victor R. Savage, Brenda S. A. Yeoh, *Toponymics: A Study of Singapore Street Names* (Eastern Universities Press, 2004).

John Steinbeck, *Cup of Gold* (New York: Penguin Books, 1995).

Angus Whitehead, "Gregory Nalpon's 'The Rose and the Silver Key': A Historicist Reading", *Asiatic*, Volume 7, Number 1, June 2013.

Angus Whitehead, "Whatever happened to Gregory Nalpon?", *Quarterly Literary Review Singapore*, Vol. 12 No. 1 Jan 2013. http://www.qlrs.com/essay.asp?id=979 accessed 12 February 2013.

Robert Yeo, "Introduction" in Yeo, ed. *Singapore Short Stories* (2. Vols) Heinemann Asia, 1978.

MEI-LIN

I HAD ALREADY BEEN ten days on the island when I met Mei-Lin. It was a small island of coconut trees and milk-white sand and, at night, a moon wide as my outstretched arms escaping from the sea.

I rented a hut there—five dollars a month. Cheap because it stood alone past the kramat° in the haunted end of the island. Nobody ever went there after seven at night. But I couldn't afford anything more than five dollars per month and I wasn't afraid except one time late at night when the earth trembled with the footsteps of some gigantic, ghostly being and the air was torn by the screaming of frightened birds. Anyway, I don't suppose I could live as cheaply anywhere else. Five dollars a month for rent, enough fish in the sea, and beer on tick° from the Chinese store. I also dived for corals° in the reef. By the time I'm talking about, I had collected a treasure of coral worth at least one hundred dollars.

And in the evenings I'd sit in the little, railed veranda of my house in the sea, listening to one of the fishermen pluck chords on his guitar and waiting for visitors from Singapore. Ah Leong, the storekeeper, had a darling bottle of old whiskey stashed away and I needed to sell my corals to buy it, the only thing in his shop that I couldn't take on credit.

I was happy on the island. The fisherfolk were friendly, the men sun-browned and strong, the women charming. We got on very well together. I managed to borrow their boats anytime I wanted and got myself invited to their homes for makan whenever my diet of fried fish grew monotonous. They lived in huts, just like mine, standing on stilts in the water. The stilts, slim and crooked, don't seem strong enough to bear the weight of the huts but the islanders say that the stilts grow stronger all the time.

At low tide, the waves seldom if ever touch the stilts, but at the high tide, the water rises to just below the floorplanks of the huts. Crowds of shellfish and crab that inhabit the barnacle-encrusted stilts crawl higher as the water rises and the sea looks green and sweet through cracks in the floorplanks.

I remember that it was evening, gold and pink and purple, when Mei-Lin came to the island. I was sitting with Ah Leong in his shop drinking beer and insulting him good-naturedly about his twelve children when we heard a heavy boat crunch into the beach and a small scream that changed to laughter. Ah Leong rushed to his wide window and looked out, and turning to me, he revealed all his gold teeth. "Visitors," he said happily. I was glad too because I could sell my beautiful branches of coral for Ah Leong's bottle of mountain dew°.

I didn't get up to look because within a few minutes of arrival, all feet gravitated naturally towards Ah Leong's store. And sure enough, I heard approaching voices as Ah Leong chattered excitedly and rubbed his palms in anticipation.

The visitors wiped the sand off their feet before entering the store. There were three men and two women. I recognised one of the men, a large fellow with a beer-distended belly who treated everyone the way he treated his favourite drink, with savour and open friendship. don't think anyone hated him. The world found him fascinating, especially women. He was sub-editor in a local newspaper and I knew him slightly. He led his party in, sweating freely under a load of filming equipment.

"Hey, bring out the beer!" he shouted happily. "I've got a thirst, real bad!" Then noticing me, he bellowed with joy and made as if to hug me. That was his way with everybody.

"Hello, Carl," I said. I gave him my warmest smile. This was a good catch. I could unload all my corals onto this man for double the usual. I made a great show of shouting to Ah Leong to hurry up with the beer, and Ah Leong, to whom I spent my earnings, reacted magnificently. Carl introduced me to his friends. There was Edward and John and John's girlfriend, Sally. And there was Mei-Lin.

They had come to the island to make a film for TV, Carl told me. Between great gulps of beer he confided that Edward and John and Sally were old friends of his and that they knew quite a bit about filming. Mei-Lin was someone he had met the night before at a party. She was a fascinating creature to whom he had been attracted immediately.

He had flirted lightly with her, and after a couple of gallons of beer, he invited her to join his filming expedition. "She's a queer one, that girl," Carl said. "She reacted with a what-kind-of-woman-do-you-take-me-for look, turned on her heel and left me. Ha! You know where she was this morning? The first one on the pier where my boat was moored!"

I took a swallow of beer and looked across the store to where Edward, John, Sally and Mei-Lin were seated. Mei-Lin sat closest to the window; a wash of sunset touched her hair, trimmed short and styled to flow around her neck, ending in two points on either side of her chin. I liked her hair. Her eyes were large; I liked them too. Her lips were soft, her throat made my teeth itch, and her cheekbones were high and strong. She wore a sleeveless blouse, her body young and firm. Very nice. She wore white shorts; her legs under the table were long and smooth and creamy, so good in fact that I wished I was a cat with short, soft fur so that I could purr around those legs. I liked all of this woman. She caught my eyes on her and smiled.

It was a mischievous, nicely naughty smile, a downright wicked thing to do to a lonely bachelor like me who consoled myself with dreams of one day meeting a woman with this kind of shape and this kind of smile. I took another swallow of beer so as not to betray the convulsive movement of my Adam's apple.

I turned to Carl. "How're you fixed up for the night?" I asked.

"Oh, any place we can hire for a couple of days," he said. And I felt a tingling at my fingertips that meant more money.

"I live alone on the other side of the island," I said. "Come, be my guests." Carl shouted out the good news to the others who, in turn, said that they were grateful for my offer of hospitality, but couldn't possibly accept it without paying me at least a little for

4

the inconvenience they'd be causing me. I protested to the contrary of course, and finally agreed to accept eighty dollars per day from them, food thrown in for free.

It was between the time of nightfall and the rising of the moon when, after a last round of beer, I walked them across the island to my hut. I cuddled Ah Leong's precious bottle of whiskey to my heart. My shrewd storekeeper friend, realising that I was in for a lot of money, had pressed the bottle on me. I will not attempt to justify my method of making money. Not now or ever. I live by my wits. And anyway, I could have struck them for more money if I hadn't been dazzled by Mei-Lin.

I made small talk with Carl as I concentrated my attention on Mei-Lin walking lithely in front of me. We passed the huts of the fisherfolk. They sat on their doorsteps and murmured greetings as we walked by. We entered the shadow of the tall coconut trees and skirted the graveyard and the kramat to my part of the island. Mei-Lin was walking beside me by then, and I acted as if I wasn't interested in her at all.

We reached my hut. It looked as cosy as closed sparrow wings in the dim light, standing alone in the open, with white-lipped waves of incoming tide swirling round its stakes.

"My house," I said, throwing out my arms.

"How lovely," Mei-Lin murmured. "Do you live here all alone?"

"Most times, except when I have company. What do you think of it, Carl?"

"Magnificent, my boy. Absolutely magnificent!"

I led them into the hut. There's a narrow room partitioned from a wider room in my hut, and a curtain of fishing net studded with starfish separating the tiny veranda from the main room. All this, of course, supported by stakes embedded in the sea. I lit a kerosene pressure lamp, tidied the place up a bit and allotted the large room to Mei-Lin and Sally, and the small room to the others. I would sleep in the little shack outside the house, which I called my kitchen.

They were a merry group of people, my guests. They went swimming as the moon rose from the sea, suddenly. And I busied myself about the kitchen. Mei-Lin was the only one who wasn't swimming; she stood by the shore watching the others. Apparently, she hadn't brought a swimming costume with her, which, as Carl said, was silly of her, but he intended on seeing her wet anyway. Then I heard a shriek, as Carl, huge and bloated as a decadent Roman emperor, rushed out of the sea and swept Mei-Lin into the water with him. Although Mei-Lin kept screaming for a while longer, I saw that she was really enjoying herself. They laughed and romped and shouted in the water, and after a time Carl and Mei-Lin, by reason of tide or current or because they wished it, were some distance away from the others, talking quietly.

I finished cooking dinner and called, "Come and get it!" and they ran out of the sea shouting and laughing. Carl led them rushing to the hut to dry and change. Mei-Lin brought up the rear. And whilst running, she suddenly changed direction, came to the shed, her clothes wet and clinging to her body, put her arms around me, kissed me with all the warmth of her young body, and then ran to the hut. I stood there, cursing with astonishment, feeling the taste of her sweet sea-wet lips on mine.

We had dinner in the main room of the hut. Mei-Lin looked at me deliberately all the while, smiling provocatively. Carl teased her but she had her eyes on me. John, Edward and Sally carried on a conversation, consisting in the main of how nice the island was and of the scenes they were going to shoot the next day. I began a series of ghost stories° after that, which made even Carl laugh nervously but had no effect on Mei-Lin whatsoever. She kept on looking at me naughtily.

Later, when it was time to go to bed, I arranged their bedding for them, wished them goodnight and retired to my little shack. I breathed a sigh of relief and anticipation. My darling bottle of whiskey! Now was the time for it. It wasn't meant to be shared. I drew the cork, savoured its bouquet, and took a nip. Glorious!

A sea breeze fanned me gently and was content. I thought of Mei-Lin when I had drunk down to the shoulder of the bottle. Supposing I fell in love with her? Impossible thought! I wasn't the type to fall in love!

But late that night, three quarters of the way down the bottle, I heard a song. A high sweet voice singing sadly. I walked into the moon-wet night and saw her leaning against a coconut tree on the beach. Without a word she came to me and caressed me and kissed me with her soft, clinging lips, and I fell in love.

She left without explanation or farewell early the next morning in a fisherman's boat. We didn't know she was leaving until she left. I consoled myself by spending all the money Carl had paid me in Ah Leong's shop. Ah Leong was rich and happy. I was drunk every day.

I took a trip back to Singapore a week later. I went to the first bar in town to see what I could do about my thirst. I picked up an old newspaper and, rifling through the pages, I saw a photograph of Mei-Lin. She wasn't alone in the photo. There was a man with her. He wore a suit and she a bridal gown. Both of them were smiling.

I looked at the date on the paper. It was the same as the day she had left the island.

Her trip to me then was nothing more than a last fling at life. I was sure that my Mei-Lin would have a happy life. I'm not so sure whether her husband would share in her happiness—but that's life, isn't it?

THE ROSE AND
THE SILVER KEY

THERE USED TO BE a rubbish heap under the great tree in Dhoby Ghaut° with a sarabat stall° parked next to it. It was a low, sprawling rubbish heap made up of the usual things—refuse from dustbins, paper, old tins and slippers and leaves from the tree above. Then one day, people forgot about it. They found a new dumping place and the old rubbish heap settled low on the ground. Time passed and its contents became warm and rich and fertile and people living in the area would take away potfuls of it to plant flowers in.

Somehow, a rose cutting, slim as a cheeping chicken's leg and almost brown, appeared on the rubbish heap one day. Rain fell, sun shone and it took root—secretly. The brownness of its stem was replaced by green. And shyly, tiny leaves appeared on the stem and grew larger, and finally a rose bloomed forth. A large red rose bending its stem almost level to the rubbish heap. The stem now had nine leaves and fourteen thorns.

A man called Hamid owned the sarabat stall on wheels—a Pakistani, tall and lean and very tough, with a well-groomed, sharp moustache, and eyes gleaming with the light of lizard's eyes.

The stall was no different from any of the hundreds of sarabat stalls in Singapore: a canvas roof, spoked wheels, aluminium counter (easy to wipe clean with a damp cloth), brass urn with compartments for hot coffee, tea and sarabat, the urn pierced by a funnel in which charcoal ambers constantly glowed, and three taps attached to the urn.

Hamid was the ordinary type of sarabat stall owner except for his shiny lizard's eyes and his military moustache waxed into two sharp barbs thrusting away from either cheek. He had large teeth stained from the juice of betel nuts°. He seldom spoke and nobody had ever seen him fight, yet no gangsters° in those times of the pin machines and jukeboxes and the Tony Curtis hairstyle° ever tried to collect protection money from him. They never presumed upon his toughness. They took it for granted in the same way as you would accept the strength of a tiger's jaw without testing it.

Soft-eyed boys, bums, men grown tired of wives' talk—all who sat around the benches of Hamid's stall respected him. He was a man of pride, strength, silence and compassion. No beggar or thirsty schoolboy° with only a bus fare in his pocket, or those who hunted vainly for a job without success, had to pay for a drink, a bun or a cigarette at his stall.

Hamid dozed by his stall every night. A carbide lamp on the stall, hissing a small point of white flame, declared that you could still buy a coffee, tea or sarabat there, no matter what the time.

He sent whatever money he earned back to his family in Pakistan every month. He had been in Singapore for eleven years and had never once returned home. He had no friends. He never allowed himself any friends. He had never seen a film. He did not read the newspapers and probably knew almost nothing about what went on in the next street because he never left his stall. He worshipped God without naming Him. If he was lonely, he never indicated it. His sole recreation seemed to be in cultivating his excellent moustache.

And then the rose appeared on the rubbish heap behind the stall, and Hamid found comfort in it. The rose was his love, his child, his God.

He gently placed used tea leaves around its stem and constantly watered it. His customers noticed his activity but none of them ever ridiculed him or attempted to pluck the rose. His lizard's eyes glowed with more intensity and the points of his moustache became even sharper with the advent of the rose. And in the evening, he smiled at Fatimah for the first time when she sat down by the stall for her usual order of coffee before starting work in the bar across the road.

Fatimah was a very pretty woman. She had long hair and wide eyes and lips like two petals of Hamid's rose. The sight of her figure in clinging kebaya and sarong always incited blushes on the cheeks of sober men. Heavy gold bangles on her wrists tinkled pleasantly whenever she moved. A silver key hung from a chain around her sweet neck. The key was made of real silver. Rumour was that she hired out the key for twenty-five dollars a time. It opened the door to her room.

Fatimah was a very desirable woman and she wasn't shy at all.

She'd shout across the road at anyone she knew. She was the cause of many fights in the bar across the road, for merely smiling at more than one man at the same time. She also displayed a small hint of inconsolable regret for her way of life, which made kind men imagine that they shared her company purely to relieve her of a weight of sin. As a result, Fatimah had collected a tiny sum of money at the post office.

She wasn't exactly ladylike, but she behaved herself at Hamid's stall. If she ever stepped out of line, it was only to whisper small invitations of promised delight to Hamid, who would sound his disapproval with a snort and a twirl of his moustache and turn away.

When the rose bloomed and Hamid smiled at her, Fatimah forgot herself and blushed. For one moment she looked like a young girl upon whom a man's eyes had rested for the first time. It was just for one moment, but then the look was gone.

"And what have I done that you are so kind to me today?" she said. "Maybe you want to marry me, huh?" Hamid's moustache quivered as he withdrew his smile. He snorted and looked away, but his lizard's eyes shone. He dipped his hands into a pail and with cupped palms he drew some water and walked over to the rubbish heap. He stooped beside the rose and let the water drain from his fingers into the plant. And he stood up looking satisfied.

The sun setting behind the rooftops touched the rose, and to Hamid it was the most beautiful thing on earth. Fatimah saw the rose and came to the rubbish heap.

"Give me that rose," she said alluringly. "Pluck that rose for me and I'll lend you my silver key for half the usual price." Hamid ignored her.

"Look at my lips," she said, "do you not consider my lips sweeter than all the roses in creation? Come, give me that rose and I'll let you taste my lips." Hamid turned away to his usual place behind the stall. The other customers avoided his eyes.

It was getting dark. He applied a match to the nozzle of the carbide lamp and it hissed into life.

Fatimah went around the stall and faced him. She reached up to her throat and dangled the silver key teasingly before his eyes. "Come, my darling man," she said, "let me have that rose."

What happened next was accepted as an inexplicable omen by many people. A ginger cat ran across the road, directly into the path of a speeding car. Fatimah screamed and covered her eyes as the shriek of the cat rent the air. When she uncovered her eyes, the car was gone and Hamid was on the road examining the still body of the cat. It lay on its side, its body slightly flattened, its eyes closed and its teeth bared in a frozen snarl.

Hamid picked it up by its tail and threw it towards a corner of the rubbish heap. Then he went back to his place by the stall and proceeded to wash the used glasses and cups.

Fatimah sat on her bench, shivering a little. A moment later she began laughing hysterically. "Look!" she shouted. "Look at that damn stupid cat!" Everyone turned to look at the corner of the rubbish heap where the body of the cat lay. But it wasn't there any longer. The ginger cat was trotting daintily down the road as if nothing at all had happened.

When Fatimah recovered herself she told the other customers by the stall, "It must be Hamid's rose that returned it to life. That rose

13

must possess remarkable qualities." No one disputed her statement. It wasn't worth the storm of abuse that would pour from her divine lips anytime anyone contradicted her. Hamid, as usual, displayed no interest in whatever she or anyone else said.

"My Hamid, I must have that rose now," Fatimah said. "I'll even lend you my silver key free of charge!" Hamid appeared not to hear her. Fatimah pleaded futilely with him, and then left the sarabat stall, shouting abuse at him as she crossed the road to the bar where she worked from eight to a quarter to twelve every night of the week, except Fridays.

It was almost eight o'clock and the carbide flame hissed brightly on the stall. Hamid served a new customer and then went to inspect his rose on the rubbish heap. Its petals seemed filled with deep red juices. Lifting his eyes, he saw Fatimah mincing her way into the bar.

A boy came with a container of rice and dhal gravy for him. It came from a shop on Bencoolen Street and the boy delivered the food regularly. Hamid paid him thirty cents from the cash drawer, washed his hands carefully and began eating with relish. Afterwards he belched in a satisfying manner, washed his hands and the container, and sat down again to admire his rose on the rubbish heap. Such a large, red rose on so frail a stem.

Hamid was content.

Customers came and went, but business was not really very brisk. At around twenty to twelve, hordes of people poured out of the Cathay Theatre° after the late show. No one stopped for a drink at Hamid's stall. They were all rushing for the last bus home.

Just before midnight, another crowd of people came out of the bar across the road. A little later, Fatimah left the bar with a group of five young men. She was laughing. They got into a fancy saloon car and drove away.

After a while, Dhoby Ghaut was deserted except for cars passing now and then. Stray dogs investigated dustbins and starlings twittered and wheeled amongst the rooftops. Hamid lay flat on his bench and, after a last look at his rose, dozed into a light sleep.

Three hours later, he wakened. He sat up, stretched and yawned. The night was cool. Someone was walking slowly towards the stall. With a spark of surprise, he recognised Fatimah.

Her hair was rumpled as though someone had tried to wrench it off her skull. Her arms were scratched and etched with weals and bruises. Her kebaya was torn and her eyes were puffed up, one of them almost closed. There was blood on her lips.

Hamid went to her and guided her to his stall, where Fatimah sat and wept silently. Hamid did not ask any questions. He made her a coffee and forced her to drink it scalding hot. He soaked a rag in warm water and wiped her face gently and cleaned from her lips the clotted blood until they became sweet again as the petals on his rose. He wiped her arms and hands and her neck, where the silver key on its chain reflected the hissing point of light from the carbide lamp. Hamid took his handkerchief and inserted it into her kebaya to cover the tear. And with a gap-toothed comb, he smoothed her hair.

Fatimah let him do all of this without a word. Her eyes were dull with the shock of how the five young men had treated her. Her bangles jingled and exploded in little golden stars as they caught the light of the carbide lamp. And she felt a strange sense of childlike wonder and pain as Hamid walked to the rubbish heap and returned with his red rose. He placed it in her hair and Fatimah wept again because she could not bear the pain of the sweetness of Hamid's rose.

Hamid drew out all the money he had° in his cash drawer and shoved it into her purse. He hailed a taxi that was passing and guided her into it and watched its rear lights until it turned a corner and disappeared. Hamid went back to his stall and sat down.

Towards dawn, as he cleaned the counter with the rag, he found the little silver key where Fatimah had been sitting. As he buried the silver key under the rose stem on the rubbish heap, he noticed that a new bud was opening into red petals. Soft as Fatimah's lips.

Of Things Magical

I CANNOT CLAIM to know a person unless I know of his beliefs. I could not presume to speak of my people unless in some way I could understand what influences them most deeply to the point of motivating their every action. I am not speaking of principles or senses of value but of the course from which principles and values spring from. I refer to the influences of the supernatural.

It is possible that the singing force that thrusts and shapes the identity of my people seeps into their souls from mosques and churches and temples, the smell of joss sticks and incense and the crisp rustle of pages in holy books. This song of faith and fear, destiny and love that affects the mind and will and the course of one's life also springs from the palmists sitting on the sidewalks in the heart of town—winning the confidence of men by relating, credibly, events of the past and charging fifty cents to predict the future. The astrologers who cater principally to mothers and fathers, charging fat fees for writing out on expensive paper the whole history, to the moment of death, of a child just born. There are fortune-tellers, old and with eyes slightly twisted, who train birds to select cards laid out in front of them (each card contains a prophecy) and men with venomous snakes that perform to the music of flute and hand-drum who sell amulets and rings and charms of great potency. A crowd gathers on a green around men like these, paying many dollars to buy oils and old bones and black wedges of cloth containing strength and wisdom and courage. These things, some of my people believe, have the power of warding off the evil of hundreds of ghosts and djinns, accidents and dangers of starvation and poverty. These dealers in magic claim that an unspeakably ugly man wearing a charm will have his features transformed to that of a handsome warrior. A man about to be interviewed for a job is guaranteed to be selected out of thousands of applicants because he wears a charm. You cannot shake the belief of some of my people in the powers of magic. Some people claim to have been rewarded for their belief in magic. Some have been cursed.

A man I know consulted a magician when he lost his wedding ring. The magician looked into a basin of lime water and floating jasmine and saw in its reflections a friend of his client wearing a ring. The next day, the friend, on being accused, returned the ring. I also know of a girl named Ruqaya, who loved a youth her parents had adopted four years before. Ruqaya loved the boy but her parents decided that she should marry another. The boy left the house and Ruqaya was married. A week later, she lost her mind. She cried and laughed and walked about, tearing leaves and papers and talking to people invisible to all eyes but hers. Her relatives gathered together and found the boy she had loved and beat him terribly, presuming that he had placed a charm on her. But Ruqaya never did return to normal. Her condition had nothing to do with magic, only with love.

Mahsuri°

I WANT TO TELL YOU of a tragedy under a tomb, three tiers tall, with the teardrop-shaped tablets set upright on either edge of the tomb. It stands in an area of wind-scattered leaves fenced with wire. And nearby, among the snarled roots of a large tree, is a small stone that marks another grave.

This is a sacred place on an island called Langkawi, off the west coast of Kedah°, north Malaya. Langkawi is the largest of a cluster of more than a hundred islands rising in close peaks of jungle. And just as a wisp of mist and mess may shape patterns of thought and, to a certain extent, control the minds of people in a narrow valley, this ancient cemetery of two graves controls all the islands—loosening an emotion of mystery and loveliness.

Buffaloes in the padi field with a crescent-horn span of five feet have eyes that speak of the quiet tomb. And the people in this island of two red buses tell their children, as their fathers and forefathers had done before them, of Mahsuri—the lady who lies under the tomb erected by Tungku Abdul Rahman°, Prime

Minister of Malaya—and of her husband under the stone among the snarled roots of the old tree.

Mahsuri was the daughter of the ruler of Langkawi. It is said that she lived sometime in the fourteenth century. She was young, and pure, and very, very beautiful. There are some old men who maintain that the orchids of Langkawi must have been touched by Mahsuri—how else could the flowers be infused with the colour of love? they ask.

When Mahsuri came of age, princes from many lands came to court her, and naturally every single one of them felt certain of capturing her love. Especially a powerful prince who was attributed with tones of evil.

But on this island, there also lived the warrior son of a poor chieftain who loved her so intensely that he trembled and felt faint every time he met her eyes. He was a strong and handsome man, and there was no warrior bolder than he in Langkawi. And it was this warrior that Mahsuri chose, above all others, to marry.

The prince who had been rejected swore to himself that he would see Mahsuri dead rather than lose her to someone else.

As the islanders rejoiced at the wedding feast, a message arrived from the mainland. The Siamese were attacking Kedah. There was no choice: Mahsuri's husband had to leave immediately at the head of a battalion of troops to defend the mother state.

After he had gone, there came to Mahsuri a long period of sorrow and painful waiting and dreams filled with swirling, slapping fear—and a premonition of terrible evil.

One day she received a message from someone she did not

know, asking her to appear in a certain glade in the jungle to receive a secret sent by her husband. Mahsuri ran, crying and laughing to a meeting place, but for a moment, the glade was empty—there was no one to meet her. Then men sprang out of hiding places all around and surrounded her and took her before her father. And the powerful prince, whose passion for her was new pure hate that boiled dirty yellow in his eyes, stepped up and accused her of infidelity. There was one penalty for her sin and the prince demanded that she suffer it. Her father could not refuse the prince's wish because it was the law at that time. Mahsuri whispered over and over again that she was innocent and begged her father to believe her. But the prince suggested that if she were truly innocent, she would shed white blood instead of red when they executed her.

She was dragged to a plain ten miles to the west of the island where a large crowd had gathered to watch her die. The prince, with her father beside him, supervised the execution. Mahsuri was tied securely to a tree and suddenly stabbed with a long, sharp kris. And everyone saw, and screamed with fear at the enormity of their sin, that the blood which spurted from her wound was pure white…

It is said that before she died, Mahsuri cursed the island with barrenness for seven generations—and the sky darkened purple-blue, and the divine fire descended to raze the padi fields of Langkawi.

I have been to the plain where Mahsuri was murdered. It is still known as Padang Mahserat, the field of Mahsuri. And here, in a place of soft earth and houses raised above the ground and wild flowers of pink and purple and white, I watched a chicken scratch up grains of charred, black rice.

A SOUL FOR ANNA LIM

OF THE TWELVE DOLLARS Samuel Paul had earned that day, washing car wheels and polishing their smooth sides until in them he could see his face—bloated and bearded, two crescents of fat pouched under his eyes—only two dollars were left. He sat in the little room in a samshu° shop, partitioned from the bar by a wooden wall with four peepholes.

The floor was black with greasy dirt and littered with peanut shells and cigarette stubs. He sat alone in the room beside one of the three marble-topped tables under a fan and a shivery blue fluorescent tube. There was a ledge of wood above his head with joss sticks and red paper and a faded, dust-caked image of a Chinese god. And pasted on the wall below the ledge, consecrated to one of the next two worlds, a girl with red hair and a stunning figure knelt on a beach of white sand, sunburnt and smooth and cool. One of her hands stretched out of the poster offering a glass of stout, the other half-heartedly tried to prevent a wispy white cotton towel from slipping down her long thighs.

Before Samuel disgraced himself and collapsed on the floor, he lifted his glass to the girl in the advertisement and drank a toast to the decline and fall° of the towel around her.

There was a postcard collecting dew from the petals of a large rose on the table among the empty bottles and peanuts and a saucer of pickled cucumbers. Samuel Paul had, earlier on, written to his mother on that postcard. He hadn't seen his mother for twenty-four years—Samuel was now 39—but he wrote to her five or six times a year. He didn't know that she had died two years after he had left her. In the evening he had written:

My dearest Mother,
Remember that I love you. To this day I carry a part of you in my trouser pocket. I have your pearl in its cage of white gold. I look at it whenever I have the time and think of you—and how much I miss you.

Greenwater Boy walked into the shop to look for anyone interested in hiring the boar that he led around in the daytime—a boar whose natural talents were dedicated to the propagation of piglets. Greenwater Boy was thirteen years old. He was very thin. He wore no shirt or shoes, only a pair of black shorts. He did not know whether or not he had a mother or father. And he could not ask, because Greenwater Boy possessed a tongue too short to form sounds that made words.

He was born dumb. He lived with Anna Lim, who did not admit to being alive. She had no soul, she said, which was why she could not accept the fact that she was alive. She said that her soul had gone, a little at a time to the first eight men who had offered her money for her company. She could not now remember altogether how many men had visited the hut in which she and Greenwater Boy lived, to play mahjong and later to take advantage of her kindness. It was a long time since she had lost her soul. The farmer who lived next to the hut employed Greenwater Boy to lead a stud boar on its business. The boy received fifty cents a day from the farmer. Anna Lim gave him a dollar for every man he brought home. He stayed with her rent-free. The dinner that she served him every evening was also free of charge.

She had found him sleeping in a bus shelter one night and adopted him. They were contented with each other's company. They worked to buy the food they ate. They looked forward to the weekends when Anna would hold their orange cat in her arms, and with its clawed paw, flick at four tubes of paper from a crowd of others on the table, numbered zero to nine. Then, opening and arranging and rearranging the combination of numbers that the cat's paw had selected, she would send the boy out to place bets on the four-digit lottery°.

Greenwater Boy yapped and trumpeted when he saw men dragging Samuel Paul out of the samshu shop. He pulled at their shirts trying to make them understand that they shouldn't do this to a drunken man. The men took no notice of him. They hauled Samuel to the five-foot way° and dumped him face down on the cold cement. Samuel began to retch at regular intervals. He hissed through his teeth and mumbled words that consisted of long drawn

26

out 'o' and 'w' sounds. Greenwater Boy waited till Samuel stopped decorating the sidewalk with the contents of his stomach. He wiped Samuel's mouth with a piece of paper and pulled him away to a place against the wall and settled himself on the floor, near Samuel's head, to watch over him.

Anna Lim waited for Greenwater Boy to bring home a customer. She had arranged the ivory mahjong pieces on the table and had set bottles of beer to cool in the icebox. She gave up hope at three in the morning and went to bed. In the darkness after she had blown out the kerosene light, she saw a black face and eyes like phosphorescent pins and two hairy hands stretching out to choke her.

She yelled and hid her face in her pillow. The hands brushed her neck and she yelled again. She turned to face it. The hands and eyes were a few inches from her face and throat.

Anna's mouth stretched tight open—her eyes bulged—her head and neck jerked and she found that she could not make a sound. Screams and sobs choked in her throat, exerting a pressure that stopped her breath. And the hairy hands and yellow eyes in the black face brushed her cheeks and throat. It growled and its lips curled over—white fangs and ribbed red gums. This time Anna closed her eyes tight, and with her face shuddering she screamed in terror and she felt the thing scream with her and she thought that she also heard the orange cat shrieking outside her window. Anna woke up a little later. She felt very cold and afraid. The room was filled with an odour of indescribable filth. She lit the kerosene lamp and opened the front door. She walked out to the path outside her window and found the disemboweled body of the orange cat. Its throat was gashed and its face was ripped open to the bone.

A parade of ducks waddled across Samuel Paul's mind as he slept on the five-foot way with Greenwater Boy sitting awake beside him. The ducks were followed by strutting cockerels and fat piglets and empty stout bottles. The boy saw a smile on the face of the sleeping man. Samuel was seeing images of the many things that he had abducted in his valiant pursuit of food. The fact that all the things he saw belonged to other people did not irritate him. It lent an air of freebooting piracy to the normally dull business of keeping his stomach filled with solids and effervescing liquid. He smelt the aroma of good things cooking over an open fire and belched with pleasure. He saw many of the hours he had spent in satisfying gossip with old women. And his hands shaped the house he would build one day—a house on a hill with exactly three casuarina trees growing around it. He breathed handfuls of breeze that a morning sea threw into his face and he became involved in a glorious sea-wet kiss with the girl pasted on the wall in the samshu shop. He felt her even teeth nibbling his earlobes and groaned with satisfaction and woke up to find a small boy tickling his ears.

Samuel Paul never suffered from hangovers. He looked around him, and gathered what had happened the night before.

He accepted the boy's presence without searching in his mind for an explanation. It was almost dawn and the street cleaners had begun their work. A few stray dogs were roaming about and the first hawkers came to set up their stalls that took up most of the road space. Samuel stood up and stretched himself till he felt a creaking in the small of his back, his shoulders and neck. He yawned loudly and wiped his eyes with the back of both his index fingers and shambled across the road to an open coffee shop. Greenwater Boy followed him. Samuel took no notice of him, not even when he sat by the same table. Greenwater Boy rested his elbows on the table and began a series of yawns, each one longer than the last. Samuel stared at him, greatly interested. The boy finished yawning and smiled widely with happiness. "Eh, eh!" he said. "Eh, eh, eh-eh, eh!"

And Samuel made his face stern and said fiercely, "Paradise is an island set in a lake of wine. You have to drink wine if you wish to travel to Paradise. Did you know that?"

Greenwater Boy smiled. "Eh, eh," he said. "Eh, eh, eh." He clapped his hands and pounded the table.

"Nothing to get excited about," Samuel said. With a slight note of modesty he continued: "Except that I thought it out myself. Anyway you should say Bravo! Or if you want more, shout Encore! Encore! Instead of whatever outlandish thing you are saying." He ordered two coffees and as he stirred the milk at the bottom of a thick porcelain cup he pulled out of his hip pocket a coloured comic strip torn from a newspaper. He spread it on the tabletop and smoothed out the wrinkles on the paper. Then he leant back against his chair, cocked his legs, balanced the comic against his uplifted knee and began to read intently.

Anna Lim had just left for the market when Greenwater Boy brought Samuel back to their house. Samuel tore off his clothes and bathed in cold water from a well in the garden. When he had dressed himself, feeling fresh and alive, his throat aching for the sweet gurgle of ice cold beer, a rope tied around his waist to keep his trousers from slipping, he found Greenwater Boy crouched and weeping over the body of a mutilated cat.

He helped the boy dig a hole and bury the cat.

"All things die, little one," he said. "The manner of death matters little. The reason for death is important. I'm sure that God has taken this cat to his own warm house. Maybe God has an excess of fish and milk and needs your cat to help him finish it."

It was sometime before the lump in Greenwater Boy's throat dissolved. He collected the stud pig from the farmer next door and led it, tugging frantically at the short tight rope around its neck, to three sows in the neighbourhood. Samuel watched with interest as the great snorting tusked boar earned fifty cents for Greenwater Boy.

When Anna Lim returned home she saw a stranger sitting with Greenwater Boy in the garden and watching the stud pig resting under a tree. She had been a petite, pretty, coquettish thing the night before. Her face was pale grey now and there was no light in her eyes. Her eyes searched the place where the orange cat had lain— and found nothing. The corpse had been buried and Samuel had washed the bloodstains off the cement with well water, scrubbing them into the drain with his bare feet.

Anna walked slowly towards the boy and the man. Samuel stood up as she approached. She stopped in front of him and looked into his eyes for a long time.

"I'm sorry," she said slowly, "I can't help anyone any longer. I can't—not after last night. I'm sorry the boy brought you here. I can ask him to take you to another place if you wish."

"I don't understand you," Samuel said. "I did not know you

lived here. The boy brought me here."

"Don't feel embarrassed," Anna said gently, the woman in her seeping into her spirit, forgetting for a moment the terror of the night before. "You see, I've no soul. My soul was taken away from me. I'm afraid that if I carry on with the business, my body also will be taken away like the cat's." She turned away from him and walked towards the house. She stopped at the veranda and looked back.

"Please go away," she said. "I'm sorry I can't help you."

Greenwater Boy ran into the house with her. Samuel stood where he was.

"God! I'd even give up booze for a woman like that," he thought. "What a queer strange thing she is."

On an impulse, he went to the pig and knelt by it and did something to its short tusks. The pig snorted and attempted to attack, but Samuel knocked it away with a sharp kick to its head. Then he went to the front of the house and called, "Lady! Lady!"

Greenwater Boy came rushing out and Anna's voice answered from within the house, "Yes, what is it?"

"Will you come out here a moment?" Samuel said. "Only a moment. There is something you should see."

Anna came out to meet him. Greenwater Boy was beside the pig, watching it toss and plough its head in the earth, trying to get rid of something stuck to one of its tusks.

"What is it, Greenwater Boy?" Anna said.

"What a lovely name," Samuel murmured. The boy held something small in the palm of his hand. He gave it to Anna.

"Oh," Anna sighed, "oh, what a lovely thing it is." She held in her hand a pearl in a cage of white gold—a pearl, pure and clear, dancing with the light of reflections in the heart of a dewdrop.

"Madame," Samuel said gravely, "I think you are holding your soul in your hand. At a time when you most needed it, a child called Greenwater Boy finds it on a stud pig's tusk. It must mean something. There must be an explanation. I think you are holding your soul in your hand."

Anna cupped her palms and bent her face to look at the pearl in a cage of white gold.

"Oh," she said—it was a whisper, a sigh, a song. "Oh! Oh!"

And Samuel Paul's fingers groped in his pocket, feeling a vacancy where he had always felt the small round hardness of a locket he had stolen from his mother twenty five years ago—a locket that he had never pawned because he still loved his mother and did not wish to forget her.

Greenwater Boy did not understand what was happening. He smiled widely, "Eh!" he said, "Eh, eh-eh!"

Timepieces

HAMID REACHED HOME late the night before, which means the very early hours of the morning, and his wife wouldn't have woken up to suggest all kinds of unhealthy things that he could do to himself if the rooster across the way hadn't decided to announce the time loud enough to startle the wits out of any decent human being. As far as Hamid is concerned, the rooster's days are numbered.

But at half past six in the morning, Hamid is warm with satisfaction and happy enough to forget his designs on the rooster. This is because he sees his four-year-old son shouting with laughter, wearing nothing but a topi and standing under the gushing standpipe, and his wife beside him heavy with child, her back straight and head held high, a slight proud smile on her lips. Life is good for Hamid: he has a good wife, a fine son and a day off to spend with them in this kampung around Bedok Corner. A bath now, then breakfast and a little stroll. The giving and receiving of greetings, a little gossip and by ten o'clock, with the sun tingling

33

warm on his cheeks, some reflections on the floods of '52.

It was a bad time for everybody in the area, especially for the hundreds of Chinese who had only a short time before settling in the low land. They had cleared the land and tilled and planted the earth with crisp vegetables, they had built a bund to keep out the overflowing of the Bedok River, they had raised ducks and chickens and pigs, they had set up shops. As Chinese New Year approached, they had established themselves on the land and were prepared for the festivity, but the December monsoon was still with us. It lasted longer than usual in that year. It rained incessantly and flooded the roads, but for a time the low lands were still safe, protected by the bund. Then on a night just before Chinese New Year, the rains increased in fury. There was a crashing of uprooted heavy trees, and then the river overflowed; a spring tide, eleven feet high, prevented the river from emptying itself, but the flood swelled whilst only little children slept.

Nine o'clock the next morning was dark and cold, and all the men and boys in the new settlement, together with those from Hamid's kampung, couldn't prevent the floodwaters from breaking through the bund and destroying the Chinese New Year harvest. The water was seven feet deep in places, and boats had to be used to rescue many people. Wooden bridges floated like rafts, bearing the few hens and cocks that had managed to save themselves, only to float downriver to the sea. And the people fought as one family to save themselves from the disaster, fought desperately and triumphed—what a time it was!

Hamid can see the settlement area from his kampung. The

river has been diverted and widened by the government. The bund is now high and strong. The livestock and crops are flourishing. The shops enjoy good business. It is peaceful and safe, not only against floods but also against communal trouble. After all, how can people who have fought side by side as they have mistrust or hate each other?

Thinking of these things, Hamid is filled with pride, an emotion that he and his neighbours deserve to feel. If ever hooligans or Indonesians venture into the settlement and kampung to stir up trouble, they will suffer the same fate as the noisy rooster across the way.

II.

The sun is low and gold on the sea by Nicoll Highway at half past six in the morning, and yet, neither the position of the sun nor the colour of the sea nor our morning light (which is a diffusion of pearl every time I've seen it) is as important as the birth of a new day.

At ten fifteen, Ng Lian Teck has occasion to tell his wife, who was supposed to have joined him at High Street three quarters of an hour earlier, that she hadn't wasted his time at all. "We've wasted so many years of each other's company," he says, "so what do a few extra minutes matter?" To the eternal credit of the good lady, let it be recorded that she chooses to feel complimented by Lian Teck's remark.

At precisely this hour, Abdullah becomes a father to his second child, a boy, safely delivered at Kandang Kerbau Hospital°, the twenty-seventh baby born this day. Abdullah is filled with joy. He is saturated with resolve and determination and has already made a hundred promises, many of which his wife is perfectly aware he'll never stick to, especially the one about coming home directly after work every day of the year. But, being kind and wise and very much in love, she understands that this is not humanly possible.

At about half past eleven, Somasundram is pleasantly surprised at his office by a gift of a fat duck in addition to a half-day off— two strokes of fortune that prompt him to buy a lottery ticket immediately. At noon, a small boy scoops up a fish with his handkerchief under the bridge across Stamford Canal,° instinctively doing one of the things any sane person ought to do at this time of the day; and at two o'clock, many people wish they were doing just that instead of having to go back to work after lunch.

By half past four, Ng Lian Teck has finally convinced his wife that he has to meet someone on a matter of utmost urgency, and ten minutes later, he is sitting gratefully alone in a nearby restaurant, his fingers wrapped around a glass of cold beer, pretending that he's a bachelor. Abdullah is on his way back to his wife's hospital room, bearing presents bought in the small gift shop. Somasundram is at home, reading the afternoon paper and inhaling with appreciation the aroma of duck curry simmering on the stove. The small boy who was catching fish under the bridge across Stamford Canal is of the opinion that grownups don't know how to appreciate the good things in life; his mother caught him coming out of the canal, smacked his bottom, and, worst of all, threw away the glass bottle of skilfully caught fish.

The moon is high and brighter than all the street lamps at

8.45pm along Nicoll Highway, and the sea slurps and sighs against the sea wall, and a boy and a girl are walking hand in hand, hoping that there isn't any more curfew and senseless fighting and threats and tension. They have too many problems of their own. Marriage has not been mentioned yet, but each of them has secretly planned it. There is a home to be established. A family to be instituted. They and all of us have a natural right to a lifetime of happiness and peace—a birthright.

III.

Margaret is an ideal name for a kindergarten schoolteacher, and this particular Margaret is a wonderful person blessed with marvellous gifts both spiritual and temporal. She has the quality of wonder, and every experience in life becomes for her quite unique, which is as it should be. She is thoughtful, kind, very tolerant and easily amused.

She is with a crowd of people at the bus stop at seven in the morning, a little saddened by an old man who speaks to another about the house of his dreams, built on a hill of close cropped grass with three casuarinas touching the sky. Margaret is amused by a young gallant who suddenly loses his composure when a little baby toddles up to him and calls him Papa.

Things are not going too well for Margaret at 8 o'clock. Tolerance has its limit, which she can't help but reach when the dog that little Ee Leng brought to class used her desk as a substitute for a lamppost. After the recess period, she finds a note on her desk that reads: "If somebody make my dog leg broken— you will die. You will die. You must pay me the dog. I'm sure you will die. You will die. You will die."

Margaret is sure that Ee Leng did not write it; Ee Leng can't even handle her ABCs. Margaret calls Ee Leng to her, but the girl bursts into uncontrollable sobs immediately and refuses to be consoled, which is a kind of distraction the class has been waiting for. The mysterious part of it is that when Ee Leng begins to scream, "You will die! You will die! You will die!" Margaret knows now who inspired the threatening note she received. But who wrote it? She may never find out.

At half past noon, she follows Ee Leng home and has a word, very tactfully of course, with the girl's mother. But things don't get on too well because the mother inquires politely whether Margaret thinks that Ee Leng is an Indonesian agent.° When Margaret tries to convince her otherwise, the mother begins to laugh. The door opens and the young man who was embarrassed at the bus stop earlier in the morning walks in. It appears that he's Ee Leng's brother, and when he hears the story, he begins laughing too and calls Ee Leng the family's 'little Indonesian agent'. There is also a certain glint in his eye that strikes great wonder in our Margaret's heart.

Much later in the evening, after the 6.30 show to be exact, the young man tells Margaret how sorry he feels for those unfortunate people who, although they are grown up, behave like little Ee Leng, spreading mischief and rumours and threats. Margaret, of course, agrees.

A Knocking on the Door

IT IS NOT FOR US to say how a soul is shaped. It is not for us to wonder whether the position and colour of a boy's eyes, the shape of his nose and mouth, the size and strength of his limbs, mutilates or in any way affects his soul. It is only a fact that Masood, eighteen years old, a boy who would be happy for hours at the sight of a bird, was born with a face and body disgustingly ugly.

People avoided Masood. He was short, with long hairy arms and an ape's face and matchstick legs. Certain people retched at the sight of him, feeling sure that he was the seed, the root and the flower of all evil. But Masood was all purity and tenderness. Masood saw no ugliness, no evil, nothing foul, in any living thing. He was an only son of a man and a woman who loved him in a way that only music can relate. Of a man and a woman who placed no faith in the mortal judgement of humans.

The man was a labourer who earned three dollars a day, and the woman was a beautiful thing, born blind. The love they had for this boy was a perpetual extension of the moment of ecstasy that a parent feels at the sight of a newborn child.

Masood had never been allowed in his life to see his image reflected in a glass mirror. He did not recognise his own image in still pools of water that he loved to peer into for the least movement of the shady silver shapes of small fishes. As a sparkle of light at night does not recognise its own beauty, Masood did not recognise his ugliness.

Masood had no friends. He did not feel the need for friends. Spring rains, young leaves and the flight of bats pleased him. He did not understand the coming and taking of men.

It can be said that Masood's conscious life was occupied with an intense longing for something he did not know. A longing which was akin to nostalgia for a place or perhaps the face of someone he had never seen. A longing that could not be satisfied.

He looked to satisfy that longing in the darkness of holes in rubber trees. He reared rats and square shell river crabs, blood-sucker lizards and ants with big heads, talking to them and searching in their form and movement for the face that he longed for. He gathered small glass bottles of raindrops and spilt them on folds of moss hoping to find in the glistening patterns a reason for his longing. He burnt petals of roses and jasmine mixed with kingfisher's wings, hoping to find in their fumes the scent of his desire.

It was almost a game he played looking for this elusive thing. His father and his mother encouraged him. They said, "Son, when you have found what you seek, you will have seen the face of God. Bring it to us when you have found it, for we also have a longing to see the face of God."

Masood felt something seeping warm in the soft marrow of his bones when his father and his mother told him this. Every day for three years, he left their hut before the blue glow of first dawn and returned only when the night insects suspended stars on the thin tips of their screams. And yet he could not find what he searched for.

His mother was a simple thing who loved any sound that fell upon her ears and every colour that her mind could imagine. But his father realised that the boy had to live alone once they were gone or when Masood succumbed to the instinct that man possesses to raise a family of his own.

"Try to look for what you want in—in the hearts of living people," his father said hesitantly. And Masood did as he was told.

Not having been in the middle of many people before, Masood did not feel the pain of scorn and insult. His smile was hideous and he smiled often. He spoke, his every sentence beginning with a "why" and a "where", but received no answer except for harsh shouted words that he did not understand.

Then Masood fell in love.

He saw her in the marketplace buying fish, and his fingers and palms and heart ached with a desire to hold and to touch her.

Her hair was a soft bundle of black cobweb tied in a bun against her neck. She had small breasts and long brown legs and cheeks that glowed with the texture of thin porcelain. Masood followed her.

With his bare feet he stepped into her footprints on the wet market floor, covering them and squirming lightly on his feet so that new forms were shaped. He stood, always three stalls away from where she was, listening to her bargaining and buying. He giggled a little with pleasure listening to her voice and imagining her whispering into his large ears.

Having bought what she wanted, the girl walked out of the market, the basket in the crook of her arm. She walked along a footpath that led to the main road. Masood followed her, smiling all the time. Little children walking with their mothers to market cried with fear and hid their faces in their mothers' skirts when they saw Masood smile. But he did not know any of this.

The girl wore a loose cotton dress and her hips rippled under the soft fabric. She crossed the main road and took another footpath that led to an acre of sandy earth and coconut trees. And Masood walked a little faster, going closer to her.

She did not feel his presence. Masood could stand just behind you and you would not feel him there. He was as clean as a breeze in the morning is clean, and his spirit was not offensive.

The girl shifted the basket from one hand to the other. She was beginning to feel its weight.

Little bubbles of laughter burst from Masood's mouth. He began to run, a long-loping stride. He reached the girl and grabbed the basket from her.

"I carry the basket for you," he said. "Come, I carry the basket for you."

The girl screamed and covered her face. The basket fell to the ground, spilling red raw meat and vegetables.

"Get away from me!" she shouted, very frightened and filled with loathing at the sight of Masood.

Masood stooped and began to gather the meat and vegetables on the sand. She shrieked and cried and kicked him and pounded his back with her small fists. Masood stood up. She choked, swallowed and spat into his face.

Three men who had been plucking coconuts ran out from behind the trees. They caught Masood and slapped and punched him. They tore his shirt and beat him with sticks. Masood fell to the ground covering his face with his hands and whimpering.

"Kill him!" the girl screamed. "Kill him! Kill him! Kill him!" The men kicked his head and his body—six strong arms with sticks, six powerful legs. Until Masood fainted.

Nobody picked him up. He woke when the moon was a silver stain in the night sky. He couldn't stand up. One arm was broken and his body and legs were terribly bruised and swollen. He began to crawl slowly on his belly. And his father, lighting up the undergrowth with a cracked storm lantern, found him and carried him home.

He bound Masood's broken arm in a splint and the boy's blind mother rubbed coconut oil on his wounds and swollen body and bandaged him with strips torn from an old sarong.

Masood moaned and muttered in delirium. He longed to whisper the name of the girl, a name he never had a chance to know.

"What happened to you, boy?" his father asked over and over again. But Masood could not say. His chest was filled with the faint presence of the girl's face and body.

His father and mother went to their own beds at about four in the morning to sleep. Masood also slept. And at about this time he heard the first knocking on the door. It sounded and stopped, sounded and stopped again. A gentle rap-rap-rap as if a large black rat, tall as a man, was balancing upright on its hind legs outside the door, tapping against the wood with its thin paws.

Masood felt an urgent need to get out of bed and open the door. He was sure that if he managed to get the door open before the thing went away, he would see the face of what he had been searching for—an image that would satisfy his queer nostalgic longing for something he could never find.

He moved in his bed. He had to get up and open the door. He was sure that whatever it was knocking out there must surely resemble the girl he saw in the market place.

The knocking stopped and sounded again, a gentle rap-rap-rap. Masood squirmed and struggled to get up but after the beating, his body felt like dead flesh and he couldn't move. Perspiration dripped into his cuts and caused a smarting that hurt like septic sores. The knocking came again and Masood shouted hoarsely. He fell out of bed and crawled to the door. He panted loudly. His bandages scraped against the knobby earth floor and loosened and slipped in coils. He managed to lift himself to his knees and raise the bolt on the door. The door swung open and a shower of moonlight was blown into the room. And that was all. There was nobody there.

His mother and father found him in bed the next morning. Masood's eyes were flecked with red and his broken arm was swollen like the bloated body of a dead piglet. His father called a woman from the village who was said to have healing hands. She came to the boy and did no more than his own mother had done for him.

That night, Masood again heard the rapping on the door like a black rat as large as a man, standing on its hind legs and scraping at the door with its paws. And again he felt the terrible desire to see the face of the one who knocked, knowing that the face would in some way resemble the face of the girl he loved.

He twisted his body and fell heavily to the floor. The rapping was louder, more demanding and urgent. Masood scraped his wounds on the knobby black floor.

"Don't go away," he moaned, "wait till I open the door. Wait, please wait." But when he opened the door, there was nobody there. And Masood cried softly, crouched against the doorstep.

In the morning his lips were blue and his wounds were caked with pus. The old woman with healing hands came from the village and rubbed his body with coconut oil. Masood did not wake. His mother forced open his lips and poured drops of warm milk down his throat. He slept right through the day and into another night.

And again he heard the gentle rap-rap-rap on the door. He did not get up this time. The knocking went on and on and he heard a voice: "Come, Masood. I have not long to wait. Come Masood. Come to me." A sighing whisper that rose and fell like a sea wind.

"I can't," Masood muttered. "I can't! I can't!" For a long while there was silence. Then slowly the door creaked open. Slowly, until it was fully open and Masood saw the face of the one who had knocked.

His mother and father went to his bed in the morning. And his father put his arms around the woman and said to her, "If only God would let light shine into your eyes, my love, you would see a strange loveliness on our boy's face." And the woman placed her hand on Masood's face, tracing its outline and seeing with her fingers. And she knew that her son was dead.

COFFEE SHOP ON THE SEA

THE COFFEE SHOP is a wooden one and it stands on the sea, which whispers and breathes underneath. It is a few feet below road level, small and compact. Its roof planks are nailed closely together and covered with zinc sheets. There are five tables inside, with round stools and a mahjong table near the door in the corner that opens out above the sea. The walls are cut horizontally in half for windows, and sheets of green canvas are rolled and tied above them to be let down when the wind blows cold with drops of rain and salty sea spray.

A counter stands in the corner of the open entrance. There is no other door except the one opening out above the sea, where it is good to stand and breathe in the salt air and see the junks and bumboats moored to stakes driven into the sea bed. A mirror is fixed on the far wall, big and broad and sometimes flattering to look into. There are two soft drink advertisements flanking the mirror, showing pretty girls with nice legs sipping their favourite drink. Shirts and pants drape the open space between the advertisements, hiding a small, red fire extinguisher and an old, cork life belt. A wire-net basket of eggs hangs from the ceiling planks. A pressure lamp, white and bright and with a big hiss, lights the drinkers sipping black, sweet coffee. And all the while there is the soft murmur of talk, like the sea talking among the stakes under the shop. This is the time when great and serious things are spoken, about business, the government, fish, love, life and sometimes about God, in a very straight, simple and sincere manner.

The plump Chinese proprietor with the smile-crinkled face and balding head always reads a Chinese newspaper. He seldom speaks; he always bows and smiles and stares intently at his newspaper, minding his own business and allowing his business to take care of him, giving him a small but definite income. A fishing net and outboard motor lean against the wall behind the counter, on top of which are a thick row of biscuits in bottles.

Most nights, the clouds above the coffee shops would be like the hard curving ribs of sand on the beach at low tide, and the stars would look out from between the white ribs.

To the left of the coffee shop, a hut was built on the sea wall like a square, squat box with walls made of uneven pieces of plank and tin nailed together. The roof is of rusty, rotten zinc and tin sheets. A long, heavy, squared-edge log had been placed outside this hut, facing the sea. And the two men who sleep in the hut at night sit on the log in the shadows and stare into the sea, listening to the sucking, squelching sound of water against the sea wall, and the slapping sweet sound as it swirls around the closely packed stakes of the wooden pier that slopes into the sea.

The blue road lights from behind them softly light up part of the sea around the stakes, and silhouette the small boats tugging at their anchor chains. They hear the sounds of the cars approaching and passing on the road behind, like the drone of beetles around a lighted lamp at night.

Old poles and planks, round and black, in all shapes and sizes, lean against the hut and lie in their own black shadow on the ground in front of the coffee shop.

The two men sit on these logs until late at night, resting completely and not talking, yawning comfortably now and then and snuggling into more comfortable positions on the log with their backs against the huts. Through half-closed eyes, they watch a man lying flat on a log close to them, busy with his thoughts. They watch the ripples of light on the black water, moving like silent music. Whether these things move the men to deep feeling or not, no one can tell. But they watch the yellow of the big ships lit up out at sea, and the old lady with short legs and shiny, baggy black trousers, who stares suspiciously at them as she passes by every night, wondering what mischief they are up to. Sometimes they smile in the shadows at the old lady, then look up at the whirling weather vane on the top of the hut spinning in the fickle breeze, so as not to meet her gaze.

From the road behind them, you can see the lighted coffee shop, the wooden pier, the square box-shaped hut and the two men in the shadows. And if you stop and look and try to feel in a little way as they do, you cannot help feeling the warm comfortable glow of peace, like a nice hot drink on a cold wet day.

IMPRESSIONS OF ISLAND LIFE

THE FAR ISLANDS, southwest of Singapore, lie embedded in a coral reef, sprouting coconut trees and grass, and mangroves creeping into the water. They are small islands, at most a few hundred yards long, quiet and peaceful.

People live on some of these islands, Malayan and Indonesian fishermen, sun-browned, wiry tough people who fish for their living. They live in huts standing on stilts in the water, tiny picturesque houses roofed with attap and floored and walled with planks. The stilts are slim and crooked; they don't seem strong enough to bear the weight of the houses, but the islanders say that the stilts grow stronger every passing year.

At low tide, the waves seldom, if ever, reach any of the stilts. When it is high tide, the water rises to just below the floors, lapping against the wooden planks. The crowds of shellfish and crabs that inhabit the barnacle-encrusted stilts start crawling higher up as the water rises. They creep up the outside walls of the huts and sometimes invade the houses. Unfortunately for the crabs and the shellfish, those that are edible are prepared for cooking; those that are not are flung back into the sea.

Most of the huts have little railed verandas that face the sea. The huts have one room only that serves for every purpose. The room is kept spotlessly clean, and often there are little cracks in the floor and walls when the planks do not fit too well. The sea looks green and cool through these cracks, when the water swirls around the stilts under the huts.

Very few of the islanders stay inside the huts during the day. The men folk are away, depending on the tide, to fish for their families. The women busy themselves with their cooking, sewing, gossip and feeding the babies. The children—healthy, brown and big-bellied—fish from the shore with long lines attached to short sticks. They play games and steal food from home, and sometimes they get spanked. They get hold of big dry coconuts and with the well-kept, sharp parangs of their fathers, they cut a third of the coconut with a bit of shell in the middle which they scrape clean. They now have the thin water-resisting skin, the bulk of husk and the bit of shell in the middle, in the shape of a shallow, flat-bottomed boat. They fix a large leaf into the ribs of two coconut leaves and stick them into the husk to act as sails. On the bottom, at the back of the boat, they pierce the skin with a sharp, flat stone, to act as a rudder. Carrying the boats under their arms, the children move to a corner on the island, where, setting the rudders a little, they launch their models and run to the other end of the island. The boats, their leaf sails bulging with the breeze, head out to open sea, dauntlessly mounting the waves. The fleet makes a sweeping turn a quarter of a mile from shore, and, just as the boys arrive, panting, at the other end of the island, the little sails come into view. Then there is a general rush into the water to retrieve the boats.

Once in open sea, five miles from shore, I saw a little coconut boat, its sails stiffly curved, effortlessly riding the waves, driving towards the horizon.

There are quiet little graveyards on the islands, under huge trees, bending under the weight of their leaves, sighing over the tiny, pointed tombstones. And when it rains, the trees cry over the graves, shedding large drops of water from the wet leaves.

On the well-inhabited islands, wooden-walled, zinc-roofed mosques are erected, into which it is impolite to enter with shoes on. To step in onto the cool cement flooring is a satisfying experience. Inside, there is a sensation of absolute peace that nothing can mar.

In front of the mosque, there is a hollow wooden log°, which is rapped sharply with a stick to summon the people to prayer.

In the morning, when the sky pinks from a little bit of sun on the horizon, a haunting prayer to God echoes over the sea in the direction of Mecca, attuning the minds of the people for the work of the coming day.

Another prayer in praise of God floats over the blood of the sea in the evening, when there is still a weak light from the scarlet sun and the banks of red and purple cloud far away.

The islanders are brave people with a healthy respect for the ghosts of the land and those under the sea, all the great variety of ghosts that they so sincerely believe in. Apart from that, they are unafraid, except, of course, when it storms, when the sky is a dark wash of cloud, dipping at places into the tense and quiet sea, and there is no breeze to be felt. The atmosphere is uneasy.

Every person on the island stops work. They stand and stare over the sea, waiting, and the children run to their mothers, sensing the trouble in the air. A slight wind ruffles the waves and sweeps, rattling, through the coconut leaves, gathering strength as it travels, until the sea is a seething mass of water. The wind grows still stronger, churning the water into a boiling cauldron, tearing the leaves from the trees. The houses shiver on their stilts.

Then a light shower of rain comes like needle-points, piercing the sand of the beach blown away by the wind, now very cold and damp, and everything is grey. It is time for the people to get into their houses, away from the angry sea and sky and the sobbing wind, listening to the swift and receding patter of rain on the roofs and walls, the wind forcing itself through the cracks, the sea seething around the stilts.

It is very dark now, and the sky is split by a crackling flash of lightning and a booming, echoing clap of thunder. Thick, heavy drops of rain hiss on the foaming sea, blanketing the surface with smoky white mist, the rain pouring in a constant, unending roar.

The people huddle together in the huts, not talking, uneasy, the children frightened and crying. The fish in the sea, upon which they live, won't get lost in the rain; the islanders' coconut trees will not be damaged, their houses won't fall, yet they sit in their huts, listening, watching, the windows and doors shut, not sleeping, shivering slightly, goosepimples rising on their flesh with the cold shafts of wind stabbing through the cracks in the wall and floor, the sea moving and violent, dashing against the houses, slashing and grinding the pebbly sands of the beach, the winds strong and softly whistling, the mist white and wet and thick over the sea.

A tormented night and the morning after is grey and tired after its exertion, like the people. The sun glows white, a little later than usual, and the business of the day goes on as before except that everything is a little damp and steaming in the sun.

With the water a little rough, the men launch their kolehs°, which they care for like loved ones, heading for their favourite fishing grounds. They fish patiently and gravely. If the catch is good, it is as it should be. If the catch is bad, Amat, who lives with them in the same house, or in the next hut, is sure to have a better catch, and he will, out of the goodness of his heart, lend some fish for dinner. The islanders are proud of their ability to raise huge sails on their kolehs, race over the sea, fleet as the wind that blows. Expert sailors, they manoeuvre their boats through intricate turns.

And when news of a race in Singapore reaches them, they train religiously up to a few days before the big event. Then the whole family, relatives and friends climb into the koleh, until the boats are inches above the surface of the sea. They hoist their sails and bowl over the almost fifteen-mile stretch of water to Singapore, munching food specially prepared for the journey, cakes and coconuts, rojak° and mee siam and a dozen other dishes, until they reach the houses of their relatives at Siglap, where the great, high-prowed, gaudily painted fishing sampans that creep down the coast from Trengganu° are pulled up on the beach.

There are a few days of rigorous practice on the sea, and then the long-awaited day of the race dawns.

A stage is built on the sand of the beach for the dance, where that night, whether they have won or lost, the islanders join in with a huge crowd of Malays for dancing and merriment, to meet old friends and kinsmen. The celebrations go on late into the night, and in the morning, after a short rest they sail back to their homes, back to the life they are used to, where everyone is interested in everyone else. Where it is good to be born, to marry and to die.

Although the government's floating dispensary° does visit these islands with doctors and nurses aboard, there is no resident qualified nurse on the island. Instead, they have a bidan°, an old lady whose speciality is childbirth. With forceps of bamboo and secret herbs mixed with government medicine, she delivers healthy babies.

Hours before a baby is born, everyone is tense, hoping and praying for the safety of the child. There is a general air of apprehension. The children giggle and run about and the men collect in little groups, discussing fish and the weather and gossip, everything except the coming event, which they are afraid to touch upon. The women are all in the house of birth, watching the bidan, who is in complete control of the situation.

Suddenly, there is a hubbub inside the hut over the sea, and above the noise of the women, a baby's first cry is heard. A new soul has been safely born on the island, a healthy boy.

When a boy reaches a marriageable age, his parents and relatives put their heads together and decide on a girl for him to marry. The matchmakers go about their business swiftly, and soon the date of marriage is fixed. Cooking and decorating is started a week before the wedding. The men, including the prospective bridegroom, erect the shed in which the husband and wife will sit in state. The population from the two islands gather in one. The children fight with each other in a way of greeting. The island seems to be crowded with cheeky, brown children chasing each other around the trees and in between the legs of the grownups.

The excitement reaches a climax on the night before the wedding, during which no one sleeps. All the last-minute details are attended to in the night and the next morning. In the evening, with everyone dressed in their best silks and sarongs, the boy and girl are married to each other. Everyone is happy, riotously happy. The children use the occasion as an excuse to be as naughty as possible. Their antics are patiently tolerated and no punishment is meted out to them. The old men discuss their feats of days long past, and belittle the present generation. The old women, gentle and ageing gracefully, gossip contentedly. The young men eye the young women, and join in the dancing. It is a happy event.

The people die as gracefully as they have lived. It is seldom that the islanders die premature deaths through violence or sickness. The people grow old pleasantly. They do their normal work, up early in the morning, working as hard as any other person. One day, when they are in their sixties or seventies, having completed part of their day's work, they go into their houses to rest, and die. Life passes away from these people without a struggle; they have lived a full life and they die with serene faces.

A death is sensed immediately by everyone on the island. The air, the trees, the breeze and the sea know it. It is announced in hushed tones, and there are sounds of subdued sobbing from the house of death.

The men dig the grave and gather planks and nail them into a rough coffin.

The corpse is tenderly bathed and cleaned with water and tears, and clothed in its best. Prayers are muttered over it; together with incantations that have been handed down from their forefathers. The body is gently laid into the open coffin. The dead person's closest friends and relatives hoist the coffin onto their shoulders and walk the little way to the graveyard under the big tree. There is no need for everyone to follow the funeral procession, the island being so small. The people stand solemnly and sadly watching the burial, and the children cry loudly for the lost one.

Thus it goes on, a little over the ten miles from Singapore°, month after month, year in and year out, the people happy and sad, sharing all their sorrows and joys, living as one in a life of slumbering content.

THE RIVER PEOPLE

THIS IS A LAND where it is believed by some that a large lizard stuffed with sawdust—its skin cured and polished, beads shoved into its eye sockets, with a still, slim protruding plastic tongue—can, in a black night ripped by lightning, come alive and roam the earth. There are people who swear by this, illustrating the fact with detailed accounts of actual experience in connection with stuffed lizards and lightning.

When mortally alive, with blood in their veins and long flicking tongues, these lizards, which we call iguanas, used to roam the banks of the Bedok River on the east coast of Singapore. This river of mud and shallow water is filled with the sound of the squelchy leaps of mud-hoppers, and the wiggle and ripple of black catfish, and the sea wind croaking among the mangrove leaves. There are crayfish, fiddler crabs with large coloured claws, and eels, which do no harm apart from fouling fish hooks, coiling and uncoiling stiffly in a terrible evil manner in the river.

And just as some people believe that iguanas come alive to the crackle of lightning in the night, the folk who live on the riverbanks believe that two spirit-people live in this river—two beautiful women dressed in misty white garments, with sweet-scented blossoms in their long black hair, who float down the river on certain nights in a fairy boat.

Although people know of their existence, they were slowly being shifted into the silver house of legend until last week.

At a quarter to eleven on a night six days ago, a taxi driver decided to stop operating along Changi Road because the sight of two ladies in a boat floating down the river like a slow leaf upset him in a manner he could not describe.

At half past eleven, the driver of a near-empty bus pulled up at the bus stop on this bridge over the river to pick up two women in white. The bus engine grumbled as it idled, waiting for the conductor to press the bell for the go-ahead signal. After a while, the driver turned in his seat and shouted at the conductor, "It's not time to sleep yet; why don't you press the bell button?"

He received a very loud and rude answer from the conductor before he realised that he had stopped for the river people.

The driver works the day shift now.

Partly of an Area of Distinguished Sea Mud

BEFORE THE STONE FENCE was erected—the sea wall stretches along that part of the waterfront where the Bugis junks are moored, up to the most famous bridge in Singapore, Merdeka Bridge—there were many wooden piers radiating to somewhere near the low water mark. There was even a coffee shop suspended on stilts above the water. And it was in this area of sea-smell and tar-smell and the talk of strolling people in the night, and the quiet of contemplative fishermen at rest, on a night when clouds were like circular ribs of frozen lard, that a patch of oozing soft sea-mud accepted the opportunity to distinguish itself.

It was only later that people knew why an old woman, with wrinkles and veins thick as worms on her skin, sat by a pier along the waterfront at two in the morning. She sat by herself with a bundle of clothes and a large handbag by her side. She stared at the sea and at the hut beside her: a square box built of uneven pieces of plank and sections of flattened-out sheets of empty kerosene tins nailed together, containing four sleeping men. She sat on a rotten long log close to the edge of the sea wall and observed the stillness and the naked masts of the tall junks and their moving, broken reflections in the receding tide. She sat at the head of a wooden pier sloping into the sea under another hut built on the apex of an arch over the pier, with a soft-drink advertisement patching a hole in its tin and canvas wall. There was a weather vane on the roof of the hut and pigeons sleeping in a soapbox beside it.

Nobody minded the old woman's business, although they saw her cry sometimes and shout angry words into the wind as her fingers tortured a handkerchief in her hand.

There were people all along this part of the waterfront, sitting, lying on their sides, strolling or standing over the sea, talking of love and politics and certain financial problems. Cars approached and passed on the road with the sounds of beetles droning around a lighted lamp. The great ships anchored beyond the waterfront were concentrative of small lights in patterns, and the small green light on the mast of a transport boat cut designs in the heavy darkness, as the old woman got up and walked slowly down the pier, crushing shrimp and crabs with her naked feet. She placed her bundle of clothes and her handbag religiously by the edge of the pier. And before the people around the place could catch a whiff of suicide, she was gone.

Then, from below the edge of the pier, there came a terrible yell of frustration; people rushed there and saw the old woman in a few inches of sea water, stuck fast in deep mud at low tide.

The old woman was rescued against her will, and it was discovered that her only reason for suicide was the state of her hair, which had been burnt by her daughter, who had tried to perm it. The patch of mud that distinguished itself was erased by a new tide and lost.

THE SPIRIT OF THE MOON

ONCE UPON A TIME, four men met in a low hut by a river-mouth after the evening prayer, to give and to receive and to share the pale fire of wisdom.

They were holy men who lived by the word of Allah as contained in the teachings of Mohammed, His prophet. And they spoke liltingly in Arabic, that being the language of the Holy Book that warmed their souls.

They were old, gaunt men to whom smiles and soft words came easily. They spent their days in prayer and meditation, and met every night in the low hut by the river-mouth to drink hot, sweet coffee and to gravely discuss things of Heaven and Earth and the subterranean kingdom of Iblis°.

They had spoken of the four angels° who bear the throne of God, one in the form of a bull, one in the form of a tiger, one in the form of an eagle, and one in the form of a man.

They had marvelled at the knowledge of the four archangels who are concerned with the welfare of man. Gibra'il°: the angel of revelation, between whose eyes is the sun, and between every two hairs of his saffron-haired body is a moon and stars. Mika'il°: each hair of his body possessing a million faces having a thousand mouths, each mouth containing a thousand tongues that entreat the mercy of God, while the tears of his million eyes, weeping for the sins of the faithful, create cherubim in his likeness who control rain and plants and fruit, so that there is not a drop of rain falling on earth or sea that is not watched by one of them.

The old men in the hut by the river-mouth had also spoken with awe of Israfil°, whose head is level with the throne of Allah, and whose feet reach lower than the lowest earth, and between whose eyes is the jewelled tablet of fate. Where would they stand when he sounded the last trumpet on the day of judgement? they always wondered. When would the eye of Azra'il° close for them? they also wondered. Azra'il: bigger than the seven earths and the seven heavens, whom God kept hidden and chained with seventy thousand chains until the creation of Adam. And when the angels saw him, they fell in a faint that lasted a thousand years. He of the seven thousand pinions. His body full of eyes and tongues, as many as there are men and birds and living things. And whenever a mortal dies an eye closes.

And sitting together at twilight as the moon soared lightly from the sea causing little waves to gurgle and slap at the sea wall, the old men felt secure in the knowledge that the angels watched over mankind, particularly at this time and the dawn when they were most exposed to danger. They were safe from Iblis, commander of the host of genies and jinns, who refused to prostrate himself before Adam.

"I prayed to Allah to give to me again the eyes of a little boy," one of them said.

"And why?" the others said softly in chorus.

"Or at least to wash away the stain of sixty years which cling to my eyes to filter the light of His beauty from my soul," he continued. And seeing in his eyes the milk of deep thought, the others remained silent with respect and waited for the words that welled up slowly from his heart. "You will remember my sister's grandson, Majid. You know that he came here to Singapore to work. And that I took him back to his village in Trengganu to prepare him for his wedding a moon ago."

The other old men nodded their heads in agreement.

"I have not told you that he is lost now. That nobody knows where he is, that madness may be in his soul. That he may have lost sight of Allah, and may be in the possession of Iblis. These things may be true, I do not know, because the wings of grief enveloped him in Trengannu and held him captive."

The sea, rising with the moon, talked with wet tongues against the sea wall by the low hut where the four old men sat huddled together.

—

Two nights before the moon bloomed full in Trengganu, *the old man who was the grand-uncle of Majid said*, shadows and light, white and cold impregnated the sea, and gleamed on the long beach where the boats were drawn. It shone on the attap of the kampung houses and twinkled in the stream that runs through the village, and silhouetted a mountain and made a sprawling furred animal of the forest on the mountain slope behind the kampung.

And Majid stared out of the windows of my sister's house whilst everyone else slept, looking at the patterns the moon drew on the earth and thinking of the maiden he would journey to marry in two days. A maiden we had told him often of, but whom, as is our custom, he had never seen.

Who knows the stirrings of his heart? But deep in the course of that night, he walked gently without a sound out of the house, down to the beach where the stream nudged the open waters of the sea. And seeing into the clear, shallow stream, he decided to follow it to its source and so tire himself to sleep.

He walked beside the stream, a stick in his hand, striking out at the reeds and grass beside it, and small things scurried and slithered away, or jumped with small splashes into the water. He walked beside the stream till grass and bushes grew into a forest on the slope of the mountain.

Shadows were dark, large creatures in the forest laced with shifting green light that slipped from leaves high above him as Majid strode on, crushing brittle old leaves with his bare feet and trying to see faces in the patterns of the moon, and he stopped suddenly, fright shouting in his heart because through the trees he saw a slim white figure moving towards him, a form that resembled a maiden, an image more tangible than moonlight.

It moved slowly and Majid, crouching by a tree beside the stream, saw clearly that it was indeed a maiden, her hair a blaze of pure silver, her skin white as milk, and the loose baju kurung that she wore, also white. She came up to the tree that concealed him, and Majid, remembering all that we had told him about the courage of male children, struggled with the great fear in him and stood to face this spirit of the moon.

Her wet lips parted softly in a smile that made her mouth desirable. And Majid saw even before the dawn of her smile—her silver hair long and gently waving, her cheeks soft and dimpled, her young body splendorous—that she was unutterably lovely.

She held out her hand to Majid, her skin so white, fairer than our chempaka° flowers, and hesitatingly Majid accepted it, her warm soft fingers entwining comfortably in his. And she led him, glancing at his face and parting her sweet mouth in smiles for him as they walked, to the little pool on the mountain slope where the stream had its origin.

And standing by the pool, which clasped a twin of the moon to its deep breast, Majid was released of his fear and asked the maiden, "Why do you favour me thus, with your presence and your smile, you—a spirit of the moon?" But she only smiled, as her silver hair, touched by a breeze, showered little stars into the night.

And Majid asked her again, "Why?" feeling in his soul a strange, roaring surge of affection and longing.

The maiden lifted her forefinger to her lips in a gesture of silence that Majid could not understand. She went to him and stood close to him so that he could smell the fragrance of her soft hair.

"I am to marry the day after tomorrow," Majid said. "It has been arranged." The maiden lifted her face to his, but Majid lowered his eyes. She drew from her mouth a rounded pebble and gently moved his lips apart to place the pebble in his mouth, where it tasted sweet and moist and warm. She stroked his cheeks softly and signed that he should give her back the pebble. Placing it into her own mouth again, she turned and went away, gesturing to Majid not to follow her.

Majid returned at dawn as I was concluding my morning address to Allah°. Lines of worry and anxiety had worked their way into his face. "And why is the bridegroom's face so troubled?" I asked.

"Do you know, Pa-Chi°, if spirits dwell in the forest by the mountain yonder?" he said.

"There are spirits everywhere, my son," I replied. "They spring even from the tears of the angel Mika'il. Every stone and leaf and drop of water and tongue of fire is guarded by spirits."

"And does the moon, when it rises, send a maiden to the earth to enchant mortals?"

"It has been rumoured," I answered. "It may be as you say, but why do you ask me that?" He did not reply. He walked away.

A terrible storm rose that evening. It wiped the moon from the sky and shattered the boats on the beach. It almost tore the roofs off the houses trembling in the kampung, and we could hear the dull roaring of the whipped-up sea and the sound of great trees crashing in the forest.

The calm came just before dawn and we hurried to prepare Majid for the journey to meet his promised bride. But Majid was not to be found, until a kinsman said that he had noticed a man battling the storm to reach the forest.

We went there with all haste, and after a long search, found Majid by the pool, holding in his arms the limp form of a maiden with silver hair and skin whiter than our chempaka flowers. Her wet clothing clung to her body and was spattered with blood, and her eyes, bright pink, were wide open and frozen in death. And we heard Majid reminding her of their meeting the night before, and of what had transpired, and pleading with her to return to life.

A girl called Ruqayah, an albino, had lived in a kampung nearby. Her hair was silver and her skin was white and her eyes were bright pink and sensitive to sunlight. She had wandered about only on nights lit by the brightness of the moon, and her mother had given her a pebble to suck so that she would not speak to strangers in the night.

But Majid did not know any of this. He held Ruqayah in his arms beside the pool into which a great tree torn by the storm had plunged, crushing the life from her as she had come in the night, in the hope of seeing Majid once more before he went away as a bridegroom.

As we took her body away, Majid wept with the slow realisation that she was a human being, and not a spirit. And with his mind painting images of what might have been, he left us.

—

The four old men in the low hut by the river-mouth discussed the matter in faultless Arabic and echoed the prayer of the one who had spoken, a prayer that Allah would grant to them again the eyes of a little boy to see and believe the wonder of the things as they are.

Two Faces

ONE NIGHT IN SINGAPORE, thirty-eight years ago, when Ahmad Jaffar was a child, he found a twisted, tough tree with a hollow at the level of his eyes. The hollow was the size of a street lamp bulb and, standing on tiptoe, he saw that it was a cave with snake-smooth walls and a flat floor of wood dust. Ahmad Jaffar scraped a piece of green moss from an old stone wall nearby and fitted it onto the floor of the hollow. He plucked small toadstools from a rotted chunk of wood and planted them in patterns on the moss. He tore rose petals and jasmine petals, and after placing the shreds on his open palms, he blew them into the hollow where they settled gently in between the toadstools on the moss. And, when the moon soaked the earth with a silver mist, he caught a shimmering dewdrop on a caladium° leaf and tipped it onto the moss in the hollow. In the morning, he rushed to see if elves had danced in the place he had prepared for them. But no one had been there—not a thing had even sipped at the dewdrop among the flowers on the green moss in between the toadstools. Two days later, he found a dead sparrow on the ground, lying on its back. Its legs were folded against its breast and its eyes were covered with wrinkled grey skin. He placed the sparrow in the hollow and blocked it up with clay to keep out the elves.

When Sulaiman was a boy, thirty-two years ago, he packed a shirt and a nice cake in a bag. Before he left his house, he travelled in his mind to a country he had read about in his geography book, and then slipped into his mother's room and kissed her sleeping cheek. He carried all his school books under his arm and walked to the beach and threw them into the sea and he laughed loudly so that the night would understand his scorn for conventional things. He walked down the road until he felt tired and decided to rest under a tree until his legs stopped aching. When he woke up, his clothes were damp with dew and his teeth rattled with the cold of the morning. When he reached home, his father and mother were still sleeping. He changed his clothes and hid like a frightened puppy under the folds of his blanket. He received a caning an hour later for losing his books, which had cost a total of $21.50.

I tell you these things about Ahmad Jaffar and Sulaiman so that you might understand the nature of their real selves at a time when they were innocent—at a time before they walked through the passage of the years like a field of wild grass, their souls like their trouser legs, pierced by hundreds of sharp yellow grass seeds which they found difficult to brush off, because they had to be extracted one by one and gently. The grass seeds were the deviated principles and ideals studding their souls, as they grew to be men in a world that forcibly changed them to what they are at this time. Today, Ahmad Jaffar is a confidence trickster still serving a prison sentence. Sulaiman is in the civil service.

Pangolin

WILD ANIMALS ARE elusive as pretty girls on a motion picture screen—and a bit more, to the point of not even showing themselves, to me especially. I experienced this frustration when after four months of periodic ventures into the jungles of Kuching°, Sarawak, I saw nothing more than a lizard, a squirrel and two monkeys. And I, who had always wanted to capture wild animals alive, had to allow my imagination to do it. And then, a wonderful thing happened.

We lived four miles away from Kuching town, the lady, her husband and I, in a place of streams, and jungle crowding the back door, and black snakes squashed by car wheels on the road and shrivelling in the sun. And small green misted mountains sloping above the horizon. At about 11.30 one night, driving home from the cinema, the strong headlights of the car picked out a shambling creature crossing the road. It was a blurred figure that merged with the grass verge as the car jammed to a stop, a safe fifty feet away.

It is not true that I was afraid, it was the dim light that made me look sick—the time had come for me to prove myself, to measure my courage and daring. I jerked the car door open and advanced slowly towards the creature, and two hearts in the darkness of the car beat loudly and prayed for my safety.

It looked like a hunched wild cat in the grass, about three and a half feet long, one and a half feet high.

Nobody in the car heard me whisper, "Shoo! Shoo!"

As I approached the beast I suddenly realised that I had never even dreamt of capturing a wild animal with my bare hands.

It didn't 'shoo'. It stood there staring at me, a miniature prehistoric monster, not a wildcat, something more terrifying, which turned slowly and began to swagger across the road. The headlights picked it up again. It was something with a thick tail like a crocodile, golden scaled, a high, humped, solid back, sloping again to a lean pointed face. Long claws clicked against the road surface, talons long as six inches and strong. It took no notice of me.

I tiptoed behind, kicked it gently and ran, stopping to see in which direction the beast was running. It hadn't run at all! It hadn't moved! It even looked a different shape. The little monster had shyly curled itself into a tight, golden, scaled ball.

I approached it again, circled it carefully, and suddenly grabbed it tight against my chest. It weighed about sixty pounds of muscle, golden scales and sharp claws that ripped the flesh of my thumb. I did not dare let go although all my nerves screamed for it. The boot of the car was opened and I dropped it in there.

When I opened the boot again, jumping away and searching the inside with the beam of a torch, I saw the poor thing huddled and quiet in the darkness. It did not move as I lifted it and placed it in a soapbox with grass and a sweet potato. It spent the night in my room, its fleshy long nose wet with yellow tears. I tried to imagine all the earrings its claws could be converted into. I couldn't sleep. The encyclopaedia told me that it was a pangolin, a harmless scaly anteater.

We sent it to the curator of the museum° the next morning, and the last we heard of the wild animal I had trapped alive was a letter from the curator.

"Many thanks for the scaly Ant-eater, (Pangolin)," it read, "It is terribly hard to keep these animals alive, but I will do my best. If it does die, it will make a very useful museum exhibit."

Michael and
the Leaf of Time

IN THE AFTERNOON, Paul washed his sampan, lifted up the floorboards, scrubbed them and put them to dry in the sun. He scaled and sliced two fishes into strips and after dipping them in black soya sauce and sugar, he ate them raw. He drank water after eating, tasting the sweet juice of the fish still in his mouth. And he walked into the sunlight, seeing sky, sea and sand, not as separate, definite things, but feeling all of them as keenly as he felt the sun on his copper skin. Then suddenly his nerves shivered like touched, taut strings as he saw the baby on the shore line, lying among weeds and soft, sea-shaped driftwood like a piglet cast up by the sea.

Paul spat out his chewed cigar and ran towards it and knelt beside it and swept it into his arms, cuddling it close to his warm, dry shirt. And he hurried away from the spot towards his hut by the river-mouth, leaving deep footprints on the sand behind him. And very gradually, clear water flowed upwards into the footprints to peep over the sand rims at Paul's old black trousers and long loose hair.

Paul talked to the baby as he walked, at least he tried talking with cooing sounds and tongue noises, but the baby seemed quite unperturbed by the situation, looking directly into Paul's eyes so that Paul looked away as an animal looks away when you stare into its eyes. And so Paul spoke to the baby as you would speak to me or I to you.

"Ay, little one!" he said, his voice softly harsh, the voice of nudging pebbles on a stream bed. "Do you come from the sea? Or did some genie leave you there for the waves to smother? Ah, the waves are hungry, little one; they draw you with long tongues into their sea belly and then spit your bones on the sand." The man walked with the child towards where the river-mouth and sea met, leaving a double row of footprints behind him. And into each one, water rose, charging them with life, and it stared and listened to the man's soft talk.

"Do you understand what I say, little one? No—how can you! But you must listen to me, you must listen because inside me my heart is rotting. Put your hand close to my heart, little one and hear what the worms say as they eat me.

"They say that I am an old man. They say that I have not lived long but I am an old man, because like an old man I count the passing of each day and I dwell too much in the past. I have no friends, little one, and I have no God and my eyes are filled with the barbs of ugliness so that I cannot see anything beautiful in anything and the wind has stopped playing tunes in my ears. It only whispers things now, very bad things. It tells me always that I saw my mother kill my father—my good father, my friend, my wonderful father—and then she killed herself. See, little one, my hair is grey because of this.

"But where did you get your eyes from, small child? Your eyes are the eyes of an animal in the dark. Maybe you are a spirit child. Maybe your mother is the moon and your father the sun. Most probably, you are a child of shame thrown to the sea to die. But I find you beautiful with your black hair and brown skin and green eyes, and already I love you."

Paul had walked a long way along the beach and sand-coloured crabs glided now like shadows before him. They reached the river-mouth and the hut that was his home, a small old hut standing on a bed of grass. Sunlight slipped off the leaves of the great tree before it played like soft balloons on the walls of the hut, old smooth planks coated with sun and rain and wind and sea smells. And standing under the great tree, Paul said, "Your name shall be Michael and I take you to be mine—to know and feel only the pure things of nature as an animal does. Never to know the rot and dirt that is in man. To live as I would have lived if terrible things had not happened to me. Come, Michael, into our house."

And Michael grew in the hut with Paul always talking to him, as a man talks to another man, so that Michael was a boy. For six years, he was a child and then he was a man, a man like Paul. Not as big, not as strong, but a man all the same. A reasoning man who understood the song of the trees and colours of the sky and the talking of the river and the ways of crabs and fishes and birds and crawling things. The fingers of his hands were so that every dying thing that he touched lived with full life. Green things that ate the sun and drank the water in the earth, things of flesh and hair and blood and bone, and things with feathers that sang songs, Michael understood. So that Michael himself became like these things, living for the same reasons as they. And Paul was satisfied. Michael grew into a young man, his eyes green and soft and fierce like an animal's and also animal-like his body, brown and sleek and strong.

Now Paul spoke to Michael about people and the evil in their natures, that they themselves were the only pure men left on the earth. Paul lied but Michael believed him, believed every word that he uttered. After all, were not he and Paul one feeling, one life, one being in two separate bodies? "Yes," Paul said, "that is so." All mankind was corrupt and evil; they were pure. Then Paul began to notice that Michael avoided meat, so he stopped the slaughter of animals for the table. This was the time when wet winged butterflies crawled out of their cocoons and flew like jewels into the sun. And for the first time, Paul left Michael many hours alone and would return late at nights to sit beside him—their forearms, thighs and shoulders touching, and feeling the warmth of each other's skins. But gradually, Michael felt that he was no longer a part of Paul because Paul was no longer a part of him. He felt sorrow at this realisation but did not speak of it. And when Paul rumpled his hair and asked if there was anything the matter, Michael smiled slowly to please Paul and said, "Not one thing."

Then one evening, Paul went out and returned with a girl, a girl so delicately lovely that Michael suppressed his sudden desire to kill Paul for propagating a lifetime of lies. People were hateful and evil, but this girl may not be like other people, Michael thought. Paul would not bring ugliness and filth into their home.

And later when she was sleeping, Paul said, "I love her Michael, as I love you. She will be a part of us as we are a part of each other. She will not come between us, Michael. She is alone and afraid. She needs us. We are still the same, Michael. Are we not indivisible?" But Michael did not answer and Paul, looking into his eyes, became afraid.

Now Michael knew that Paul was no longer a part of him, set apart from Paul and the girl, and Paul did not attempt to renew the old relationship. He got a job at the sandpit a couple of miles away and worked there the whole day. Meat appeared on the table again, and after some time, furniture and fancy ornaments from town decorated the hut. Michael felt a wave of nausea every time he saw Paul, so he avoided him. But not the girl; she, he could not avoid. Her name was Mu-Lan, and Michael was completely aware of her beauty when he kissed her the first time on the beach at twilight, and from then on lived in a state of tortured rapture and doubt. He took to sleeping by the sea at night and writing, before the first waves of incoming tide, her name on the sand in letters twice his height. And as the sea sighed across it, smoothing the sand and taking her name into its deep heart, he would murmur that he loved her and ask the sea to love her as he did. He would hear the *thrrr* of the birdwings in his half-sleep and whirling thoughts that formed and faded in his mind and the lingering sweetness of the night before—these were mornings. And afternoons were sunlight and the sea and peace.

Days dissolved into weeks and months. They were happy times for Michael.

Then, on a night that was damp and mist, dimly lit by cold stars, Michael was standing alone on the shore where sixteen years before Paul had found him, and a place of darkness took form and lurched along the beach towards him. He heard a thick voice calling his name and recognised Paul. And Michael went to him. He saw that there was dirt and blood on Paul's shirt and it was torn and his eyes were half-closed and his breath smelt sharp and sour.

"Sit with me, Michael," he said and flopped down heavily on his haunches. "You and I have not spoken for a long time, Michael. It is time for me to teach you more of the things of life." Michael squatted beside him but not too close. Paul tried to rumple his hair but Michael avoided the hand. "What have you been doing to yourself, Michael, avoiding me, huh? I know. For a time, things have not been the same. Not as they used to be when you and I were a part of each other."

The sea hissed along the sand as Paul spoke. "It was all because of that woman, Michael. She was cheap and unworthy of love. What is love, Michael? Love is a dirty word, a barrel of filth smeared with honey. The honey's been consumed—the filth is all that's left." Paul began to cry and Michael struggled to control nausea and flaring anger. "You and I are one, Michael, only you and I. Oh Michael, I respected and loved her and all the time she was carrying the child of another man! Only you and I, you and I, Michael. We are pure.

"My mother killed my father. I killed Mu-Lan. I broke her bones and snapped her neck and threw her into the river. I killed her—*I*

81

killed her—do you hear me Michael?" Paul lifted up his head and shouted, he stood up and tore open his shirt and beat his chest, "I KILLED HER for you, Michael, so that we can be one again."

Michael's hands groped for a stone, a flat sharp stone. He stood up and with the side of his palm, he chopped Paul on the neck, his muscles almost bursting out of his skin as he punched. Paul collapsed, whimpering with fear and pain. Michael knelt on him and stabbed him with the sharp stone. Paul screamed. With one blow Michael smashed his teeth, and then jabbed his eyes out. Paul lay quiet on the sand, his lips shaped words: "You and I are one, Michael. You and I are one…"

Michael was breathing heavily with strain and the pain and the pure hate singing in his blood. He lifted his hands high above his head and stabbed down with the stone into the big, throbbing vein in Paul's neck.

Water in the deep footprints on the sand looked over the rims at Michael carrying Paul slung across his shoulders, staggering towards the river-mouth. The water in the footprints, coloured with fresh blood, was happy as prophets are when their prophesies come true, as it watched Michael fling Paul's body in the river-mud and turn his back to the hut and the life that he had lived, walking along the river bank to the main road—to join the people and become a part of them.

A Box Labelled God

PEOPLE THOUGHT THAT the problems of Dustin Rias, complicated threads of doubt squirming in his mind, were nothing more than excuses that he invented to avoid the respectability of a steady job. Dustin, actually, was not satisfied by the ordinary reasons for a steady job. He had first to find a purpose in life. He had found none so far.

This was a time when his cheeks were flushed with the blood of youth.

One night at around this time, his mind became an open place of dream, with a cold flute note that peaked and collapsed into the shriek of unclean things somewhere among broken mountains, and thick puddles of blood bubbled beats of newly forming life as Dustin woke up, shivering with terror.

He lay awake until morning trying to understand the dream, and he decided that it was not really a dream but matter that had leaked from hidden places in his own mind, a revelation, a glimpse of the birth of time and life.

Every night from then on, Dustin left the house of his parents and went to the sea to squat by the mudflats, there to contemplate on his vision. Sitting by the oozy mud and waiting for the foam and roll of the sea, he tried with concentration and will to force from his mind the missing fragrance of the dream. He tried desperately to squeeze from his mind that part which contained an image of God.

Dustin finally decided to become an ascetic. He left his house, and his mother assumed a pose of resignation that concealed the absolute relief she felt. She offered two candles on her altar and prayed that it would be many years before she saw Dustin again. He had been living off her long enough, she thought.

The first thing that Dustin did upon leaving the house was to go to a bar, mix his drinks and get pleasantly drunk. After having achieved this, he saw a girl with soft brown hair and a nose that was dented on the bridge. Her lips were full and her body, plump to the point of ripeness, shifted under her silk dress as soft as though fingers were constantly stroking it. He spoke to her. Her name was Teresa, she said. She was a woman who had never regretted a single thing in her life. She believed in God and the saints and the powers of darkness. Dustin thought that she was altogether a wonderful person. Her eyes seemed always damp, and she breathed out her talk, which touched Dustin like an exquisite pain. He did not love her with the intensity of infatuation; he only knew that he would be comfortable and happy with her.

He did not realise that he really needed her until he had built a hut. He chose a place by the river mouth near the mudflats. He gathered driftwood and dismantled a rotting shed half a mile away to build the hut. It had one room, a little kitchen and a wide window, with uprights planted to support windows and floor and attap roof. But at nights, all of the heavens seemed to shine into the room.

After green creepers had been trained all along the windows of the hut and a garden planted, Dustin invited Teresa to join him, which she duly did. She washed and planted and cooked and served his food, whilst he occupied himself by the mudflats and tried to force fragments of God from his mind. After a while, she began to nag at him, but Dustin did not mind.

One day, a small boy poked with a stick along the mudflats and was suddenly caught by Dustin, who held him by the lapels of his shirt and began raving. "Listen small boy, I want to shout, to yell, to climb the highest swaying tree and let the news slip from my lips like gold into the wind. Listen. Listen. Her elbows are plump and dimpled. Her body is filled with a baby. She is so lovely—"

"I must go home," the boy said.

Dustin began to work for the first time in his life. He washed and gardened and cooked. He fished and swept and fixed the leaks in the roof. He did a hundred small things that made Teresa happy. A smile of maternity could be found more on his face than on hers.

"Ah, what you are giving me, Teresa, is more precious than gold or God," he almost sung. "As soon as the baby comes—hell! before it comes, next week—we'll shift into town. I'm giving up all this nonsense. This is my purpose of life, to work for both of you. We'll move into town and I'll get a job. Damn it! Let's go to church and get properly married!"

But two days later, as they were preparing to shift into town, Teresa had a miscarriage and Dustin felt himself die inside.

He did not cry or curse or blame anybody, not even God, for what had happened. For months he moved from the hut to the mudflats and back. He shuffled about the place, never speaking. His mind mumbled indistinct things. He seemed aware of nothing.

One night, a long time later, he screamed in his sleep and cried until his pillow was saturated with tears. He wept without waking and Teresa held his shuddering body in her arms until morning.

The next day, he walked to the closest village, half a mile away. When he returned, he said to Teresa, "I've got a job. You can have clothes and money and all that you want to eat. I will work day and night to provide for you, but you must give me a son." And that night, by the mudflats under the stars, he said to himself, "I have not gone about my search in the right way. I must see God before I die. I must have a son who will show me the face of God, a son who will be a continuation of me, my blood, my mind, my soul. A son who will begin the search for God as soon as he's old enough, without going through all the things that wrecked me even before I began."

Dustin worked as a labourer, sweeping drains and emptying dustbins. Every day, he bought from the market all that Teresa needed, and for himself a bottle of cheap samshu, which he drank by the mudflats every night. Finally, Teresa gave birth to a boy. Dustin had a look at it and announced that its name would be Baptist. Teresa did not argue because Dustin had kept his promise to her, so it was right that he should have the privilege of naming the boy.

Sixteen years passed and Teresa grew fat in awkward places.

Dustin stuck to his work and drank samshu by the mudflats every night. Baptist grew tall and strong. He was not sent to school, but Teresa taught him how to read, to write, and to avoid hurting people. Baptist was the kind of son that mothers dream of but seldom get.

One night, Dustin asked Baptist to sit with him by the mudflats, and in the soft darkness, listening to the ripples of waves resting at the lower water mark, Dustin spoke to his son. "Boy, have you ever wondered why you are alive? Why we all are alive? Why we are happy and unhappy, sick sometimes? Why people live to grow old and die?"

Baptist did not answer so Dustin continued. "It has been said that we were created by God. I want to see the face of God, son. Think of it. If someone could see the true face of God, he could tell the whole world about it. Hell, son, if someone could describe the face of God, why, we'd be in paradise again.

"Boy, I've taken care of you all your life. Now you must go and do what you were born for. Leave us and go and find me the face of God. Go home, pack your things and leave tonight."

Far out in the darkness, the first waves invaded the mudflats, and Baptist wept quietly. The breeze plucked at some of his tears and flung them on Dustin's face.

"Go, son," Dustin said gently. "We all must accept our individual responsibilities. You were born for a purpose. Go and fulfil your mission in life." Baptist rose quietly and walked towards the hut. He did not look back.

Teresa did not know of what had happened. She wanted to

contact the police the next day, to register Baptist as a missing person when he had not come back, but Dustin stopped her. "He has gone to do what he has to do," he said. "We have no right to stop him."

"But why did he run away? I took care of him. He was happy here."

"I sent him away, Teresa, to find me the face of God. He was born for that purpose."

Teresa did not speak a word. Her mouth tightened and her eyes grew hard. She packed her things and left the hut that night.

Time passed slower than the dissolution of mist threads at dawn. Dustin's hut sprang leaks and slanted, and the uprights supporting the hut rotted. Dustin cleaned filth and emptied dustbins with an air of dedication. Every morning for ten years, he visited the small post office in the village and asked if there was anything for him. He always received a negative reply. Then one morning, the postmaster handed him a square parcel wrapped in brown paper labelled 'God'. The sender's name was Baptist.

He took the box back to the hut and a hundred speculations roared and quarrelled in his mind. His hands trembled. He was absolutely certain that the box contained the face of God. He tore off the wrapper and saw revealed a white cardboard box, the kind in which cakes are delivered. There was a letter resting on it. He opened it.

Dear Father, it read, *I did not understand you on the beach ten years ago. I think I hated you for what you did. But now I bless you. Inside this box is a particle of God and yet all of Him.*

Look into it, and with a little reasoning, you will see the face of God. Mother is with me and she is well. We hope you will come and live with us. Your son, Baptist.

Dustin lifted the lid of the box slightly, just enough for his hand to slip in. His fingers groped around the inside of the box and brought out a cigarette. There was nothing unusual about it; it was a normal, common cigarette. He laid it reverently on the table and put his hand into the box again. This time he drew out a miniature bottle of whisky. He put it beside the cigarette on the table, feeling afraid because he could not understand what he was seeing. He threw open the lid of the box and peered inside. There was a crust of bread wrapped in wax paper, and a photograph of a laughing, plump baby. Scrawled in Baptist's handwriting at the foot of the picture was one word: MINE. The last object in the box was a twig, a dried, brittle twig with dead leaves and a hump of a caterpillar's cocoon stuck to it.

Dustin stood staring at these things. His head began to hurt with the effort of analysis. The sun slid down a curve in the sky and began to burn the colour of blood, and on the twig there was an almost imperceptible movement. Very slowly, the shell of the cocoon on the twig began to flake and crack, falling away in scales. And painfully, it seemed, a wet-winged butterfly emerged from the cocoon, resting on the twig until the sun slipped below the level of the hut window. Its wings quivered for a moment, then, like twin silvers of a fragile jewel, it flew out of the window, leaving Dustin to the darkness of his hut.

Dustin gathered the pieces of the face of God and placed them back into the box, then he went to the mudflat and squatted there, still as an old stone idol, until the blue-silver light of dawn softened the whole world.

THE APPOINTMENT

THE PALM OF MY HAND assured me of a long life, one woman to love, children and much happiness. And I did not doubt it. That is why I stirred awake this morning, hearing her sigh in my mind, my heart taut with expectation. We were to meet today, at six in the evening at the sea front where the coffee shop used to stand on stilts in the sea. Her name is Carol and I love her. It's been five years since we last met.

Christmas was longing and pain for me. A bottle of whisky helped me through yesterday. And every minute before six this evening was barely tolerable. I hadn't seen Carol or phoned or written in five years.

I reached the waterfront an hour before the time of the appointment. I had taken to drink since we last met, but as much as I needed it today, I didn't touch a drop of the stuff. I thought I could give it up if I had Carol with me. I was sure that I could do without gambling and fighting as well.

I walked to where the coffee shop used to be and waited for

Carol. I was dressed in my new Dacron° wool suit, and I wore a yellow Siamese silk scarf loosely knotted round my neck. I had just this morning shaved off my beard and bathed myself in light eau-de-cologne. The odd little donkey that she had stitched stood comfortably in my coat pocket; he wore tight chequered trousers and quite an inconsolable expression. I remembered that with a drop of Chanel No 5, we had christened him Nikki°. Would Carol remember that? I wondered. And the songs and laughter, the retelling of what we dreamt each night, the patterns she saw in bars of sunlight on grass, the recording of Lecuona's *Andalucía*°, and the violin of Ruggerio Ricci° playing at two in the morning. Would she remember? Mornings were always green-gold for us, and nights soft, secret shadows. Noon was a time for sleep and evenings were stories for children who clustered around her. Would she remember? It was not really essential for her to do so. If she would only keep her appointment with me, I would tell her softly of all these things and of how much I loved her, my Carol.

I would tell her how she had grown into a part of me. She knew of course that I had tried to pluck out that part of me and found that I was wrenching at my soul. That was when we had made the appointment after the separation of five terrible years. The intensity of my passion for her would not tolerate the gaze of any other man upon her. Listening to the chatter of evil men, I doubted her virtue. I could not live with myself loving and hating her at the same time. I tried to destroy her love for me by spreading scandalous untruths about my name—crushing her love like a flower only to feel its thorns pierce my heart. "Go to the dogs if you wish," I told her exactly five years ago, "dive into the pit of hell if that is your desire. I will return in five years to wash you and claim you for my mate—if you haven't been taken by the devil by that time!" You see how I felt? In agony of pain and love and doubt, for the last time before I left her side, I smashed a porcelain vase on the floor when I asked her to tell me again that she loved me. And she remained silent, her head resting on the table and her hair reaching down to the floor, masking her face. I'd known that she was weeping, but in my anger I felt no pity. I had been seeking desperately for peace that I would not allow myself. I realised now that I had to confront myself and prepare a fitting house in my heart for peace to enter with soft wings, secretly.

I thought Carol knew this when she let me go away from her side. I knew now that she had believed in me and loved me and had tried to tell me of the man who had betrayed her many years before I had met her. But I would not hear her talk of it. I believed that she was quite innocent of the ways of the world and condemned her for distortions of the truth that I had heard from other lips.

Waiting for Carol at the waterfront this evening these thoughts thrust themselves into my mind. Where was Carol? I was filled with doubt and worry. People were strolling past me, slowly, peacefully. Drizzle, light as sea spray, was falling, and a couple walking with a bright-faced child called out the compliments of the season to me. Would Carol forgive me? Could she disregard the hurt I had caused and learn to love me again? Did she have another man? Was she married? Was I a presumptuous fool?

The rising sea slapped and gurgled at my feet and I thought

I heard Carol's voice shouting my name. A merry voice calling, "Kenny! Kenny!" I raised my eyes quickly to catch a glimpse of her. There were more people pacing the waterfront now, but she was not among them. I was not surprised. It was not six yet, and I had heard her voice many times over the years, heard as in a dream calling me, and the familiar sudden ache in my heart. How does a woman affect a man so?

The peal of cathedral bells° reached me faintly. Solemn bell sounds floating over schools and shops and the large hotel to reach me. They were not the bells of Christmas. They were slow and sad bell sounds, a funeral knell.

Then a soft hand touched me and light perfume seemed to drench my heart as I turned to face Carol. It really was Carol come with a smile beside me! I did not care for the people around me. I put my arms around my Carol and held her to me. My heart pattered crazily as I squeezed her in my arms, never wanting to let her go. She was crying and whispering my name over and over again. I buried my face in her hair, not daring to speak for fear that I should also weep. She stayed in my arms for an eternal moment. Then she drew away from me, and I saw that she was laughing and crying with happiness. "Kenny, Kenny," she whispered, "how are you, Kenny?"

And all I could do was blurt out "Merry Christmas!" and hold her to me again. It was Carol I was embracing! My own dear Carol, holding her in my starved arms. And I told her that I loved her, wishing that the word was more adequate to describe my feelings for her. But she sobbed and shivered in my arms and clutched me as if we were never to see each other again as the cathedral bells tolled the knell of death. I was suddenly afraid.

"What's the matter, Carol?" I asked. But she shook her head in reply. I kissed her and wiped the tear stains off her cheeks. "Carol, darling, what is wrong?"

She tried to smile at me. "Nothing, Kenny," she said, "I'm feeling cold. Let's walk a little."

We walked along the seafront with our arms around each other's waists. I suggested that we go to a café where we could get something warm to drink. But Carol said that she wanted to walk along the sea as we used to before. The cathedral bells did not relent their mournful toll and I noticed that Carol winced as if in pain or fear at every bell note. "There is something wrong, Carol," I insisted. "What is it?"

Carol's face was calm as she answered me. "We won't be able to see each other again, Kenny."

"But why?" I cried.

"Hush, my dear," she said, "We have only a few moments left before I have to go. Say that you love me."

Words of sudden pain, but she put a finger to my lips and shook her head. "I love you, Carol," I blurted out. "I love you more than my heaven, my god or my life."

Again Carol shook her head and put her finger to my lips. "Never say that of heaven or God or life, Kenny," she whispered, as the church bells tolled their tale of sorrow.

"I must go, my darling," she said. "Don't stop me or follow me. Never doubt my love for you. I have kept my promise to meet you here today. I'm sorry that we cannot spend the rest of our lives together. Oh, Kenny, I love you!"

"Let's get married, Carol," I begged. "You don't really have to leave. I won't let you leave me! Carol! Don't leave me. I'll make you a good husband, I promise!"

Carol's eyes glistened with tears as she lifted up her face to be kissed. I crushed my cheeks against hers and held her, pleading with her not to leave me. For one moment, her young body was tight in my arms and her voice was clear in my ears as she whispered goodbye and blessed me, and then in an instant she was gone! I did not feel her disengage herself from me; it was as though she had suddenly vanished!

I looked around me but could not see her. "Carol!" I cried, my voice a shouted sob. "Carol!" No one answered, except the cathedral bells singing of death. "Oh my God," I whispered. Were they pealing for my Carol?

I ran like a madman to the cathedral. They were bringing out a coffin to a waiting hearse. I saw her parents and relatives following the coffin and I knew that my Carol was dead. But how could she have met me if she was dead? I felt a stab of hope! I rushed to her father and clutched at his sleeve.

"She died of cholera this morning," he said gently, tiredly. And I thought I heard her voice calling over the sound of the bells from a great distance away, over the sound of the bells, "I love you, Kenny! I love you…"

THE GRASSHOPPER TRAPPERS

THE LABOURERS CUT GRASS near noontime along a country road in Singapore. They were blackened by the sun and gleaming like polished ebony in blue singlets and khaki shorts. Dirty handkerchiefs were tied gypsy-fashion around their heads. Showers of green grass flew into the air and settled in the hollows of ears and down sweat-wet singlets where they itched. The air carried the scent of sliced grass and the crunch of sickles tearing grass and sometimes the spark and sharp snick of a sickle striking a hidden stone. As the labourers earned their daily pay in the sun, small Malay boys trailed after them, staring intently at the flying pieces of grass, looking for almost invisible green grasshoppers.

Each boy carried a slim bamboo rod at the bottom of which a net was stretched tightly across the face of a wire ring six inches in diameter. Cylindrical wire-mesh cages hung from their belts. And inside these cages, crowds of grasshoppers clung to the walls looking at the flying grass with eyes of dull grey shell.

These boys rear birds at home—birds that they trap with a

boiled solution of latex and rubber cut from old shoe soles. They spread the gum along the fragile stem of a single coconut leaf and place it in the known haunts of cuckoos and green pigeons and singing morboks°; a morbok bird may be sold for anything between five and two hundred dollars, and even more, depending on the tone and quality of its song.

The grass by the roadside is long and sleeping before the touch of the labourers' sickles, bristles stiff and short and alive as the blades pass through it. And the boys, who may possibly earn more than the labourers, kick around the cut grass, watching the grasshoppers leap and settle. Then a wooden rod will flick out, and a grasshopper wriggles under the taut net against the ground. A boy's hand gropes flat along the grass, creeps under the net, secures the stiff springy insect, and transfers it into the cage hanging from his belt.

The boys go home near noontime with their cages full, their netted rods resting like fishing poles on their shoulders, to feed the cuckoos and green pigeons and singing morboks, while the sickles of the Indian labourers slash incessantly at the long grass.

THE ONE-EYED WIDOW
OF BUKIT HO SWEE

THE ONE-EYED WIDOW once had a hut near the temple at
the summit of Bukit Ho Swee° in Singapore, having lived there for
twenty years. She had five children and they never had enough to
live on, especially since her husband had died three years ago. Her
eldest son worked in a box factory. He earned two dollars and sixty
cents a day. One daughter worked in an old oil factory, the other
in a paper factory. Each earned one dollar and sixty cents a day.
The youngest son went to school in Kampung Ho Swee. One more
child stayed at home.

On a night last July, their hut was outlined for an instant in
a wash of flame and they ran with a screaming mass of seven
thousand five hundred people away from the fire. Now they live in
a Singapore Improvement Trust° flat near Bukit Ho Swee. It has a
red door, grey walls, cream windows, a sitting room, one bedroom,
a kitchen and a toilet. The cement floor is cold, scrubbed clean

and bare. With the hundred dollars that she received in relief aid, she bought a kerosene stove, a meat safe, four stools, slippers for everyone in the family, hot pans, porcelain bowls and a square area of linoleum for the bedroom. There is nothing else in the flat. It has the cold emptiness and smell of never having been lived in, as if nobody alive stayed there.

In the centre of the bedroom, nesting on the bare linoleum are the only two articles saved from the fire: a sewing machine perched on a wooden trunk, standing high and quiet like an altar to a pagan god of destruction. The signs of the one-eyed widow saved the trunk. The police recovered the sewing machine and four ten-cent coins from the site of the fire.

The one-eyed widow and her family lived in the flat rent-free for three months. Now they have to pay fifty-five dollars a month for rent. There is only one breadwinner in the family, the son who works in the box factory; the factories in which her daughters had worked no longer exist as they exploded in the fire. The school where the youngest boy went also burned. The old widow had fallen many times as she rushed away from the holocaust. She is afraid to walk now; she cannot explain it, but she trips and falls all the time.

THE HUNTER LAYS DOWN HIS SPEAR

THERE IS A SITUATION of employment, non-employment, gainful employment and gainful non-employment here and everywhere.

The slaves of Egypt who built the pyramids, and the Africans who raised the cotton in the American South were employed for those tasks.

Their reward was whipping, starvation and death. But they were employed.

Employment means to use the services of others and to keep them at work. Work means an expenditure of energy.

Man was the hunter, the provider; the meat that he returned with on his shaggy shoulders in prehistoric past was his only obligation to his family, and he rested in the knowledge that he had been employed. He subsisted and was happy with the thought of it. This is now not sufficient. We have forgotten the element of rising expectations that has caused turmoil in the economic measures of the major nations.

Man now wants and needs not only the meat but the profit that goes with it.

Rising expectations! Utopia! Shangri-La? No! He has learned to move from the sweatshop to a deserved and dignified place in his weak life.

His strength is buttressed by his inherited tradition of free demand for his rights as a unit in society. He wants his share, and to hell with the wheelings and dealings going on in the stock market, the sale and use of arms, the embargoes that cripple the synthetic structure of the world economy.

Man is still the hunter and he must have his meat for the family. He must and does aspire towards the goal of a house, a TV set, perhaps a car. And what about the children? And a little money to be put away? All this comes from the job. The employer is one who has to design and cater for the programme of rising expectations if he is to avert economic horror.

If man is not employed, the sense of dependence upon another is lost. He would be more secure in a feudal system of which there is none, and under which he would not now live in any case.

There is then the host of the gainfully unemployed. The hunter in many nations has laid down his spear and depends on society to feed him. He receives his dole, his unemployment benefits. And in receiving this social hand-out, he emasculates himself.

For man, the hunter, the dot in humanity, he has heard too much flatulence emitted on the subject of employment through various media.

He has heard that we are now reaching a saturation point in employment. But because of circumstances out of his control, he is retrenched. He receives compensation. He looks for another job. He returns all property due to the finance company. His head is bowed and he is ashamed. His children lose their respect for him. There are no more rising expectations. Only the seeds of despair and the embers of revolution.

There are people in Singapore who will recognise and exploit this situation. Employment agencies that field out 'experienced' workers, typists, telex operators, stenos, accounts clerks, etc. solicit clients through hard-sell operators. Aware that the unemployed desperately need work, they set their terms.

"Fill in your time sheet correctly." That appears to be all right except for the fact that the hours are trimmed by the agency to exclude overtime.

"Hours after 6pm and after eight working hours are calculated for overtime."

Which means that even if you have worked 12 hours, you receive no overtime till after 6pm, which is accepted by the worker even though he knows that the Employment Act° says that this is an offence on the part of the employer.

Your remuneration amounts to a paltry one-third of the fees charged by the agency. On the average, food alone consumes most of this income. You try to subsist. What price rising expectations?

If the Ministry of Labour° could effectively be of service, if it could take over the operations of these bogus and deceitful employment organisations and offer respectable service to the unemployed at a reasonable profit, then man the hunter will rise in the expectation of life.

THE MANGO TREE

PEOPLE WHO LIVE FAR AWAY from towns seem born with understanding and respect for all things around them. They do not wonder how things came to be or why, because they know of these matters. They inherit explanations for the existence of each and every thing. They recognise the existence of natural and supernatural forces.

They did not know how old the mango tree was. It grew in the centre of a long slope of grass. It was a tall tree with a thick, gnarled trunk, and its branches grew in distortions so that the outmost tip of each branch was never far from the main trunk. Its long leaves were coated with a gritty black fungus. Fruit appeared from amongst its leaves at odd times, especially when mangos were out of season. They were tiny fruits, hard as stone and they always fell weeks before the time of ripening. A stranger slept under the tree one night; in the morning, people found his dead body hanging from the lowest branch of the mango tree, his swollen tongue black as one of its fungus encrusted leaves.

At that time, only five families lived anywhere near the mango tree. They lived in attap houses built far from each other so that even a scream could not span the distance between the houses. They farmed the land, which was ten inches deep with black earth so rich that tapioca roots grew uncommonly fat, each a yard long. The people reared goats and chickens. And they kept singing morbok birds in intricate cages.

They respected the mango tree. One day, an old woman heard a puppy barking as she passed by the tree. She looked around her but could not see any pup, although she could still hear the sound of its barking. Raising her eyes, she saw a black puppy with blood-red eyes and teeth long as knives, sitting on the topmost branch of the mango tree and barking down at her.

After that, the people hammered seven long, strong nails into the tree trunk and confined the spirit dog° to the upper branches of the tree.

Five months later, a truck branched off the main road and climbed up the slope to the mango tree. It was loaded with beams and poles and planks and attap. The driver and three other men unloaded all of this under the tree and drove off. One man stayed behind. He selected four poles and a crossbeam, and with a hammer and nails, some attap and planks, he built in exactly three weeks a lean-to against the tree. His name was Awang. He was 42 years old. His shoulders were broad, his chest massive and his arms thick with writhing cords of muscle. The house had a kitchen and a veranda and a large rectangular room in between.

The mango tree now grew from the centre of the main room,

lit by wide windows. The apex of the attap roof ended below the lowest branch of the mango tree so that from a distance, in dim light, Awang's house looked like compost heaped neatly around the trunk of the high, black mango tree. Awang fashioned tables and chairs for the house. He built a cooking place in the kitchen and a low platform to serve as a bed in the main room. Behind the kitchen, he dug a deep well. He went away the next day and returned with a woman and a little girl, and also three goats and squawking hens and two roosters.

His wife Minah was a plump, comfortable-looking woman. She had a great capacity for laughter, love, and hard work. She had borne Awang only one child, a daughter named Ruqayah. Minah often hoped for a male child, a son for Awang, a brother for Ruqayah. A male child who would grow into a man, kind and strong as his father, and who would respect them and care for them when they were old. A man who would bring children of his own blood to the house built around the mango tree.

Ruqayah was a pretty child. She was 10 years old. She was a strange and happy girl, and knew of everything there was to know. "Stars balance on the tips of songs sung by night insects," she would say to her mother, who enjoyed listening to her talk. "And every time an insect dies, a star falls from the sky." Every passing thing filled her eyes with wonder. And thinking deeply as she helped her mother to cook, wash, sweep and sew, she would learn the secrets of many things that our eyes accept without question.

On their first night in the house, after they had bathed and eaten and lit the oil lamp hanging from a nail on the mango tree, Awang said, "Has this house told you any stories, Ruqayah?"

"Not yet," Ruqayah said, "it doesn't know me yet. The house is shy now. When it has lost its shyness it will talk to me."

Minah giggled happily. "I think I will get very fat in this house," she said. Awang smiled. After talking a little more, they went to sleep. They were very tired.

Late that night, Ruqayah went to her father and shook him awake "Pa!" she whispered.

"What is the matter, child?"

"Pa, the mango tree talked to me just now. It said that it was lonely and sad and cold."

"All right," Awang said. "The next time it talks to you, ask the tree what it wants and I'll see what I can do. Now go back to sleep."

Awang always treated seriously whatever Ruqayah told him. He felt that children knew more than grown men or even old men. And so, before sinking again into sleep, he thought of what Ruqayah had told him and resolved to do something. How good it would be to have two children, a boy and a girl; sometimes Ruqayah would say things that frightened him just a little.

Awang hoed and planted the next day, on a plot of land at the bottom of the slope. He dammed the stream beside the road and widened a part of it to make the beginning of a fish pond. And whilst looking for firewood in the small forest across the road, he managed to capture an iguana. Awang trussed each pair of clawed legs together with two pieces of string. He looped and knotted its long, writhing tail to its hind legs and carried the reptile to the house. Its forked tongue flicked in and out of its mouth hopelessly all along the way. It was a young iguana, only two and a half feet long.

Awang built a low, square fence around the trunk of the mango tree, in the room. He untied the iguana and placed it within the fence. "See!" he said to Ruqayah, "I've brought a friend for the mango tree. He will scratch the tree with his claws, and soothe it with his long tail, and warm the tree with his rough skin."

Ruqayah was satisfied. But she wept bitterly for the tree, when she found the iguana dead the next morning. Its throat was torn as if teeth sharp as knives had ripped it open. During the night, Ruqayah had heard the snarl and bark of a puppy.

"It must have been a dream," Awang said, "or a stray dog barking from the roadside." But Awang himself could not explain the state of the iguana's throat.

Time passed and Awang and Minah became acquainted with their neighbours. Awang's hens laid eggs and hatched chickens. His goats bred kids and were heavy with milk. His vegetable patch yielded crisp leaves and fruit and fish grew fat and sluggish in his fish pond. Awang prospered. Minah was so fat by now that she found difficulty in pleating her sarong.

Ruqayah was taller and prettier, now 12 years old, and the trees and birds and animals spoke less often to her. She was of that age when she felt the beginnings of scorn for the kind of talk we call childish.

Minah was teaching Ruqayah all the cooking recipes her own mother had taught her. Bent over the cooking place in the kitchen, Minah spoke to Ruqayah of womanhood. Minah spoke as if she always talked these matters over with Ruqayah. She spoke as her own mother had once spoken to her, softly, of the miracle of life and a man's needs and a woman's joy; of love and pain and family. And Ruqayah, listening, felt a slow rush of wonder and joy, the first magic of womanhood.

The mango tree brooded over the house. Small, hard fruit falling prematurely from its branches had, on one occasion, struck holes into the attap of the roof. Awang spent half an hour repairing it. From the distance, in late evening, the house looked even more like compost heaped neatly around the base of the mango tree than it had looked when new.

A neighbour had already approached Minah for Ruqayah's hand. Minah spoke to Awang about it but he felt that Ruqayah should not marry until she was at least two years older. And even then, she should marry an educated man—a teacher, maybe, not a farmer. Awang planned to add an extra room to the house. In idle moments by his vegetable patch, he would draw designs on the earth with a twig. He wanted to make pieces of furniture exactly like those he had seen in town.

Over the next two years, Minah was approached by fifteen different mothers whose sons were stricken with love for Ruqayah. Awang found none of the men suitable. Ruqayah had grown into a lovely young woman, shy and bright-eyed, waiting in expectation of a man her father would approve of. The extra room had been built, the furniture made.

Then, as though it was always meant to be so, a distant cousin of Minah's visited them. In the evening before she left, the distant cousin asked whether Ruqayah had been promised to any man. She had a son, she said, a student teacher. Would Awang and Minah accept her son as Ruqayah's husband-to-be?

Awang was content. Minah wept as mothers do when they are truly filled with happiness, and hugged Ruqayah close to her. Many things had to be prepared for the wedding.

Ruqayah heard whispers of loneliness and cold and sorrow that night. If she were younger, she would have said that the mango tree had spoken to her.

A month later after the music and feasting, the laughter and the helpless tears of old, fat women; after repeated blessings and the departure of the fifty-one guests—deep in the cool night, Awang and Minah heard a scream of terror from the new room. Ruqayah rushed out of the room, still screaming.

Minah caught hold of her but Ruqayah struggled desperately against her mother. "The dog! The dog!" she screamed. Awang ran to the new room. Ruqayah's husband lay on the bed, his eyes bulging, his mouth stretched open in a frozen shout of terror, his throat ripped open as if torn by teeth sharp as knives...but there was no dog anywhere in the room.

Ruqayah had stopped screaming when Awang turned back to his room. He saw Ruqayah with her arms wrapped tightly around the gnarled mango tree trunk. Minah was trying to drag her away from it.

Ruqayah was stroking the tree with her cheeks and lips and neck. "Oh, I love you, I love you!" she whispered, "All my life I have loved you, without ever having known you. You are the reason for my birth and my life, Oh, my husband, I love you…"

The mango tree still stands on the grass slope and people staying far away from the town treat it with respect, as they treat all other things. There is no longer a house like a compost heap around its stem. Awang dismantled it, taking away its planks and poles and beams, and with it, his wife Minah and his daughter Ruqayah, now quite insane, taking them to the town where they had come from many years ago—far away from the mango tree.

GENTLEMEN OF LEISURE

ESPECIALLY DURING THE early night hours, if you dress in yesterday's suit of clothes and walk into the streets moving as if you had nothing particular in your mind, if you shuffle into coffee shops or sit quietly alongside some sarabat stall with eyes gentle and uninquisitive and ears ready to listen sympathetically to any story, if you move further on into soft lights, warm near the cold of the harbour, or to the parks in places glowing with the talk of first love, you will meet gentlemen unlike any others you may have known.

You will know a gentleman of this variety by his talk, which will begin with a casual greeting—"Are you well?" or "Have you eaten?"—a greeting to you purely because you are a man and alone and therefore, automatically, a friend. This greeting is sincere, unlike the conventional, "Hello, how are you?" which has no meaning because its proper significance has been lost long ago. The man is only too willing to share a bun, a cigarette or a cup of coffee with you. And if you are not well, then he is eager to discuss the particular disease from which you suffer. He will tell you of his many friends who have been sick the same way, of their discomfort and the great pity in his heart for sick people, and he will remember a foolproof remedy concocted by somebody's mother-in-law. Later on, you will discover that he has convictions on anything from God to politics. He minds his own business most of the time, and he knows how to avoid hurting your feelings.

You may feel that he is working you up to a point when you would gratefully lend a sum of money, and you are puzzled when he doesn't ask for a single thing. Looking closely at him, you may be surprised to see that he is still a young man. A healthy, contented person. Yes, but wise beyond his years. Then you will ask politely, small details about his occupational life. He will hesitate, and then an amazing story filled with romance, adventure, and sweet sorrow will tumble from his lips, about a business liquidated on account of an insincere friend, oh! a most insincere friend!

But on the whole, things are quite all right nowadays. Very soon, he will be accepted by a large firm, and then, who knows? Maybe he'll find a nice girl and settle down.

The Americans call this kind of a person a Bum, the English a Loafer, and the police sometimes address them most rudely as Vagrants.

We shall call them Gentlemen of Leisure.

I am speaking of true things about people I know. And since many of these gentlemen are young men below the age of thirty, I shall tell you of how they came to be this way.

It starts off in school. A rebellious boy argues with a teacher and decides to leave, or sometimes goes right through school often tasting the sweet feelings of unbounded frustration. The boy, out of school, has never thought of a career and now his parents insist that he get a job.

Anyway, he looks up the situations vacant ads in the newspapers, half-heartedly posts an application and is surprised when he's accepted. It's not that surprising actually, because this kind of person has qualities of courage and intelligence above the average. Well, after a few months of being pushed around, he chucks the whole thing up or is dismissed, swearing that he'll never work again. He goes out into the streets, having learnt to look up to no man as a superior or to treat anyone as a subordinate.

Now, as he moves freely, undisciplined and even without a home (because parents seldom tolerate this kind of behaviour), he is not yet a gentleman. Now is the time to prove that he can withstand the shrivelling, stabbing pain of hunger, to go without the cigarette his nerves scream for, to make good friends and keep them. Now is the time when, as his bones harden to the feel of bare stone or sand at nights, he learns to respect age and wisdom in any man. And slowly, he rises up in the world that he now views with a most impartial air. He has very good friends who need someone to help them in their little shops or fishing boats, and for a little while each day, he helps them. After all, a favour done to someone cannot be considered as bribery, even if he makes a little money, or better still, cigarettes and something to eat, maybe even a large fresh fish—after all, there's nothing tastier than a hot fried fish dripping in its own sea juices, especially as the air at night turns cold around the harbour.

From this time on, there are no more problems in the life of a gentleman. Every day that dawns is the beginning of a new happy life, to live, to use and to shape to one's own satisfaction. His circle of friends ranges as wide as the world. He is no longer being pressed in the tight noose of dissatisfaction and worry over promotion, position, hypocrisy and forced friendship for business reasons.

This business of friendship can also be embarrassing sometimes even to a gentleman of leisure. I remember one day when a showy character, who disliked the police on a matter of principle, met a gentleman.

"You come with me to Katong, man, and we'll have a good beer," the showy fellow said.

"What's wrong with a beer in town?" the gentleman said.

"Oh! I've got small trouble in Katong, you can help me settle it and I give you a beer."

So the gentleman went to Katong to help the friend. He had a beer. And half an hour later, the small matter that his friend had come to settle came up in the form of eleven gangsters armed with parangs and bottles and sticks—which goes to prove that even a gentleman has to be wary about his friends sometimes.

Now you must remember that this is still the testing period—it takes at least five years of this kind of life to produce the picture I described at the beginning, and during the first few years of his new life, love plays a very important part in the life of a gentleman. These people fall in love in a most deep, dramatic and magnificent style, always with a lady most pure and cultured with a very homely charm.

And always the affair is purely platonic and unrequited. It is borne and treasured and meditated upon until a marriage is hoped to be announced in the papers on parental pressure. But then, strong with the feeling of having been betrayed, the gentleman vows that for always onward, for as long as the sun shall shine and crickets scream, he will be a bachelor with a beer bottle as his first and last love. Love is sweet pain that a gentleman is ordained to suffer. Marriage is not.

Religion is, of course, not necessary in this kind of life. Some sort of organised belief however is vital. All through his life, the gentleman speaks lovingly and simply of God, who, he is sure, looks kindly at poor people and forgives the repentant sinner's valour of thought, which deflects the sin of presumption. And as the man grows older, God is his only refuge and often the pit his only pleasure. But then, how can God forgive a man who has not sinned?

The path of a gentleman is littered with pitfalls. We have dealt with love. Now we come to one other: the feeling of lassitude, the feeling of not wanting or doing or crying or anything, sunk into a complete space of depressing emptiness, like being on the inside of an old shoe. A gentleman, if he is to survive, has to be interested in everybody and everything, genuinely interested, or he will perish in this state of lassitude in which he sees no point even in eating or drinking, but stumbles around toad-eyed and very soon dead. The fight against this feeling fires these people, the gallant qualities of honour and charity and understanding and every gentleman of the kind I speak of has survived this fight.

Now you must not confuse the true gentleman of leisure with

some other people who call themselves gentlemen but who are actually victims of circumstance. Starting the same way out of school then set upon by individuals who exploit their fine senses of comradeship and adventure by snarling them into secret societies where they are used as tools to collect protection money and— Oh! Hell! It's fine for them to feel that all so-called members are brothers sworn to avenge or go to the aid of any other member. Maybe a sense of self is derived from strutting around the chicken yard of other people, but it all winds up in the total extinction of the individual that is sometimes hidden by long hair.

The boys get their pocket money, their hair styled and new clothes paid for. If arrested, bail is sometimes paid and a good lawyer engaged. But there is so much blood, and smelly yellow cowardice in their persecution of innocent people. Always the knife in the back, always the cheating and the fear and weapons to maim and kill. And finally, trapped by a tightening circle of distrust and bile, the weeping mothers and the police sweeping like hounds for the kill…

No—these are not the gentlemen I speak of.

The good people, the true gentlemen, whom I don't know why are considered useless, actually do a tremendous good for themselves, proud of their independence and self-sufficiency. They grow old like wine: mellow and mature and sweet. Humble and wise, they dream of a little hut and good friends, a warm, full stomach and a good cigarette. The brewery also has much to thank them for.

The disadvantages of being a gentleman of leisure are many and quite disheartening. For example, if a man is dedicated to this sort of life, he can never truly fall in love with a lady, because he cannot afford it and because very few ladies will look to this kind of a man as a prospective husband. So this man must live, a lonely bachelor, loving everybody but no one in particular. He may love friends who love him and are true to him, but they always go away, or get married or something. He must never allow himself to be attached to any particular person or object, nothing that he can't carry with him. He has to hear the scorn and pity of many people who once knew his family and old acquaintances, who despise with sermons.

He has to accept age and weakness and sickness in a resigned manner. He has to face the fact that nobody will be near him when he dies. But a man like this is aware of these things. He does not possess anything, so he has nothing to lose. Insults he can settle with his fists. And he can rise above sneers and pitiful chatter by ignoring them. He does not attach himself to any person because he knows that he will only be a burden to that person, and he does not want to burden anybody out of love for them. His philosophy of death is cool and wise. He will accept death as he accepts every passing moment of the day. Being, as I mentioned before, religiously inclined, he will most probably accept death, whether on the road, in the hospital or poorhouse, as a new awakening into eternal life. In his old age, as he plays with children that pass by, or act as advisor to young people; the man to whom pride and honour mean so much is satisfied with the knowledge that he has lived a full life, free, without giving or enduring insult and always being true to himself. And like the bubbling of good things inside him after a dinner pipe, he will remember with happiness all the little fine and naughty things he has done. And certainly when the sun shines for the last time upon him he will be recognised by his God and by his few friends of long ago as a true and proper gentleman.

THE COURTSHIP OF DONATELLO VARGA°

IT MUST BE REMEMBERED THAT Donatello Varga's father had once told him, "Listen you li'l rascal…choose the sweetest star in the sky and stand under it every night. Make a hollow with your palms and wait under the star and long for it and say good things to it. Ha! You know something? That sweet star is going to stay right where it is! Up there in the sky! But if you stand under it long enough, you will find in the cup of your palms a li'l pool of starlight …so boy, don't forget that!"

This kind of talk may have influenced Donatello, but it didn't do his father any good.

Donatello stayed with his mother in Newton. They rented a room there. His father stayed somewhere else in his own house with a big tree in front of it. Donatello's mother wanted no part of her husband. Maybe it was because his breath was always an advertisement for the cheapest samshu in town. Or because he was convinced that every pretty woman in Singapore owed him a certain amount of love, which he felt justified in claiming after his fifth glass of samshu. Trouble was that after his eleventh glass, he'd feel a wave of tenderness and longing for his wife. She would always lock her door to him, and he'd stand outside shouting out his love for her and weeping pitifully. But she had no sympathy to offer him. Donatello's father accepted the sorrows of the whole world after his thirteenth glass of samshu. After his fifteenth glass he felt a divine call to protect the rights of every man.

One night, enraptured by this emotion, he sloshed kerosene over a sleeping night watchman in Orchard Road and applied a match to his beard. Donatello's father is now serving a nine-year sentence in Changi Prison. It was just after his conviction in court that he told Donatello that he should stand under a star and collect a little pool of starlight in the cup of his palms; that was five years ago when Donatello was fourteen years old. And although Donatello accepted his father's parting words seriously, he could find no significance to them.

Donatello Varga had two ambitions in life. One was to be admired by the whole world, as Fabian° was. The other was to be a great trombonist like Gerry Mulligan°.

No one admired Donatello, except little boys to whom he would boast, so that listening, you would imagine that he was the most daring of men and the greatest lover since Casanova°. Actually he had never fought anyone in his life and the presence of a pretty girl would reduce him to a state of speechless embarrassment.

Donatello was happy whenever some rich Chinese person died.

He'd play his father's trombone at the funeral for six dollars a time, followed by a sumptuous dinner and two large, cold, bottles of beer. It was a good price for the wheezing bray his trombone would produce every time he tried to blow like Gerry Mulligan.

Donatello appeared taller than he actually was because of the wads of cardboard he stuffed into his shoes. He was quite pleasant to look at, if you could disregard his missing front teeth° or the thick grease in his hair that melted as soon as he walked into the sun, oiling his forehead and ears. He talked as he imagined Fabian would talk and walked with an exaggerated swagger. He collected empty packets of an expensive brand of cigarettes and would fill them with cheap cigarettes, so that anyone could see a packet of high-class cigarettes in the pocket of his transparent terylene shirt and also a crisp one dollar note which he never spent. He wore a gold-tinted wristlet with his name embossed on it: Donatello Fabian Varga. A photograph of Brigitte Bardot°, in her most kittenish pose, peered out of the cellophane window of his wallet. He'd flash it carelessly in crowded places, and smile quietly, acknowledging the admiration he thought he saw in everyone's eyes.

He combed his hair whenever he found a mirror. He'd raise an eyebrow and shape an aloof sneer with his lips whilst gazing at his reflection, and say to himself, "Huh! You handsome hunk of a man!" He practised kissing for ten minutes every morning, on his pillow, in readiness for the day when he would devastate lovely women with his kisses.

Donatello had three friends; Harun, the headman of a gang in the area whom he ran errands for; Albert, a final year seminarian;

and Dai Kee, the conductor of the Chinese funeral band. For some reason, nobody else, apart from his mother and small boys, tolerated Donatello Varga.

One day, as he was relating fabulous exploits that he had thought up the night before to a group of small boys, one of them said, "My brother told me you're a big bluff! He said you're a lousy, stupid bluffer!"

Donatello was deeply hurt. "Go and tell your brother," he said sternly to the small boy, "that I'll bash him up. Man, I'll beat his brains out. Tell all your brothers that."

He delivered this challenge exactly as Fabian would have done it. Then he turned his heels and slouched away, feeling sad that the small boys had lost faith in him, and also feeling afraid that their elder brothers might accept his challenge to fight.

He had seventeen dollars in his pocket at the time. He was saving money for a lilac coloured dacron suit and a blood-red silk shirt. But having lost all his admirers and facing a number of severe beatings from their brothers, Donatello discarded the idea of the lilac suit and blood-red shirt. He felt like investing in a couple of gallons of ice-cold beer. He couldn't go to any of the bars nearby; word of his challenge may have already spread. He took a bus to Robinson Road° to the Midnight Bar and Restaurant.

It was a cool dim place with soft cushioned seats, tropical fish in aquaria, green fronds in the corners, and lights like coloured berries in the ceiling.

When Donatello's eyes became accustomed to the light, he chose a seat and sank into its softness. There were only a few customers in the bar. It was still early in the day. The waitresses sat together, chatting gaily. One of them, noticing Donatello, left the group and hurried over. She leant over his table and looked enquiringly at him. "A large beer," he said, and became himself again, Donatello Fabian Varga, hero supreme, ladykiller, debonair man of the world. Oh, she was a lovely thing, this girl. She was fair and shaped like some fragile statuette from Bali. Her lips were red and wet and smiling, her eyes large and shiny, her hair a careless wraith of smoke stroked gently over her ears. She wore a kebaya of black lace clinging to her body and her tiny waist, and a red sarong pleated so that one smooth ankle showed as she walked on high heeled slippers coloured gold to the bar to fill his order.

Donatello wondered whether what his father had told him could be applied in some way towards the conquest of this girl. He rehearsed what he'd say to her as soon as she brought the beer. He thought of leering at her and saying, "You got anything in mind for tonight, baby?" No. That wasn't good enough. How about, "Hi honey. I've got plans for just you and me tonight! Let's go out and have a ball, oh, you cute chick, you!"

The girl came back before Donatello could make up his mind. She sat next to him, placed a glass on a beer mat in front of him, and filled it from a large bottle of cold beer. She smiled at Donatello. He blushed and lowered his head. He couldn't think of anything to say. His heart thudded in his chest so violently that he was sure his shirt fluttered to its rhythm. She edged closer to him. Donatello took a gulp of beer and choked. The girl stroked his back soothingly with her cool hand. Donatello could feel her long red fingernails

125

on the skin of his back. He could also feel the sudden rise of all the goosepimples his skin could muster.

He muttered a protest.

"Why handsome, don't you like it?" she asked softly. Donatello jerked away nervously and squeezed himself against the wall. The girl laughed, "Are you really scared of me, a big man like you?"

Donatello wished he could remember all the things he had rehearsed for just this kind of situation. The girl edged closer to him, and the goosepimples rose on his flesh again.

"What's your name, handsome?" she whispered. Her eyes seemed to sparkle with little lights. Donatello blushed. He tried to answer her but the words stuck in his throat. He took a large swallow of beer. This time he didn't choke. He braced himself for the effort and stammered out. "D-d-d-donatello."

Her smile widened and her eyes softened. "That's a beautiful name," she said dreamily. "You know, some boys call themselves Ricky or Fabian or Elvis or Cliff. They're ugly names. But your name, Don-a-tell-o…it's just like music."

Donatello immediately decided to drop the Fabian part of his name. It wasn't his real name anyway; he had borrowed it. He took another gulp of beer. "What's your name?" he asked.

"Oh, it's not as nice as yours. My name's Alice." Her name fell on Donatello ears with a sound sweeter than a chorus of porcelain bells. Alice filled his empty glass. "Another beer?" He nodded.

"All right, sweetheart, I'll be right back." She smiled at him, playfully blinked with wide eyes, and hurried away. Donatello's heart shivered in a frenzy of emotion. He felt a tremendous desire to do something great and noble for Alice.

"You know, you're a very nice boy," Alice said after she had brought a new bottle and filled his glass and sat so close to him that he could smell the scent of her soft black hair. "I don't think you can help being a nice boy with a name like yours."

"I'm not a boy," Donatello said, more confident now of himself. "I'm nineteen".

Alice laughed gaily. "All right, old man, I'm eighteen, unmarried, and very, very lonely for a handsome devil like you."

"Y-you mean you're not married?" Donatello stammered. "Don't you have any boyfriends?"

"Oh millions of them," she said, "and all of them swear that they love me."

"Then why don't you get married?"

"Not a single dog in the pack wants to marry me," she said. "Do you want to marry me, sweetheart?"

Donatello did not believe her. What she said just couldn't be possible. But there came to him the realisation of the great and noble thing he would do for her. He would get her a husband. That's what he'd do! He would find a good man to marry her so that she'd grow plump and happy and have many children.

"I'll get you a husband," he blurted out, "would you like that?"

"Oh, you're sweet," she said, smiling at him and, for a moment, tightening her fingers over his. He drew ten dollars from his wallet and handed it to her.

"I must go now," he said, "keep the change."

Donatello stood up and Alice allowed him just enough space

to squeeze past her. "I'll be back this evening," he said, "I'll bring a husband for you."

"Goodbye, Donatello," Alice called after him. Anyone who looked closely would have detected a mistiness in her eyes.

He walked out of the Midnight Bar and Restaurant. He strode like a man. He had quite forgotten his usual swagger. He was not aware of the ten-dollar note that Alice had slipped into his back pocket as he had squeezed past her. Donatello was filled with resolve and determination. He was going to get a husband for Alice.

He took a bus back to Newton. He remembered that he might have to face a number of fights. But strangely, the thought didn't bother him. He could think only of a husband for Alice. There were three choices: Harun the gang leader, Albert the seminarian, and Bai Kee the conductor of the Chinese funeral band.

He went to see Harun first. "Nothing you can do for me today," Harun said tersely. "Get lost!" Donatello took the hint. Anyway, a man like that couldn't be good enough for Alice. Albert was at home on holiday when Donatello asked him whether he wanted a lovely girl to be his wife, Albert patted him good-naturedly on the back and gave him a short sermon on the beauty of celibacy. Bai Kee couldn't help either; he had three wives already, he said, and he neither had the money nor the inclination for a fourth. As it was, three wives created enough hell for one man. "In fact," he told Donatello, "I wish I had never married at all."

Donatello Varga was a desperate man by now. There wasn't anyone else he could ask. He collected his trombone from Bai Kee and walked all the way to the waterfront. He played low mournful notes on the trombone, thinking deeply all the while. Even a tugboat's grunted answer to a trombone note didn't draw any response from him. He wondered how he could apply his father's talk about pools of starlight to his case.

Night fell on the waterfront and Donatello Varga roused enough courage to do what he had to do. He entered the Midnight Bar and Restaurant cradling his trombone under his arm. Alice spotted him immediately and joined his table.

"Hello," she said. " I expected you earlier."

"I was busy," Donatello said.

"Oh, you poor dear," she crooned, stroking his arm. "Did you bring that trombone to serenade to me tonight?"

"Alice…" Donatello said, then found that he couldn't say what he had resolved he would say. Alice saw his difficulty.

"I'll get you a beer," she murmured and hurried to the bar. Donatello felt very ashamed and afraid. Ashamed because he had not kept his promise to her and afraid because he was obliged to make compensation which might not please her.

Alice came back with the beer, filled his glass and sat close to him.

"What's worrying you, sweetheart?" she whispered. She looked so cool and so lovely that he had to swallow the tightness in his throat. He looked away.

"I haven't brought you a husband," he muttered. Alice was silent. *Oh, the poor thing,* she thought. *He really meant what he said.*

"That's okay!" she said after a while.

Donatello made an effort to control his nervousness. "Will you m-m-marry me?" he stammered.

Alice closed her hand over his. Her lips parted slightly and her eyes grew wet. "Of course, you idiot," she said huskily. "Didn't I ask you in the first place!"

Late that night, the elder brothers of the small boys went out to look for Donatello in answer to his challenge. They finally found him sitting by the waterfront. Alice lay snuggled lovingly against his shoulders as he blew low, peaceful notes on his trombone. Donatello and Alice looked so happy that the boys decided to leave them alone. Any man who could get a girl as sweet as Alice deserved respect.

A Man Without Song°

IT IS SAID THAT there are no songs in man. Only children make songs and visions and they are not afraid of shadows. I know that my friend Thiam Soo, even when looking at his fine wife and five children, has become a man.

He has lost his song. And it is possible that you will shortly read in the papers that he has executed his stated intention of burning down his father's bee hoon factory° in Upper Thompson Road. He has just emptied crude sump oil from the engines and liberally distributed over two thousand katis° of bee hoon packed for delivery.

I was there when the radio car came at his father's request. No arrest was made. His father was more concerned about preserving property than destroying his son. He told me: "As long as I have life, I give him life. When I go, he will not exist, nothing will exist for me. He calls me a fool and says that I do not wish to be a man. Let him be a man then!"

My friend Thiam Soo was born in a small room in the makeshift, attap-roofed factory in 1938°. His father rejected the servitude of a common labourer in another bee hoon factory 1.6 kilometres (a mile)° away, and come to this place beside the temple to build his factory with wood begged and borrowed and engines and pulleys and fan belts that he had scoured from every junkyard in town.

He still cannot fully grasp the written word. But with a twig and a tuneless whistle through his teeth he would improvise marvels of engineering stretched on a patch of sand. His wife had liver and sugar and sesame oil and brandy°, and her stomach was bound° when she was convalescing in the shuttered room after Thiam Soo was born. He had some pigs and a vegetable patch and he worked alongside his three labourers. He used sawdust for fuel to cook his bee hoon, and on long trestles of bamboo that he made himself, he used the sun to dry it.

There used to be snowy egrets in the fields then. Around the factory there were wild duck and snipe, little monkeys and iguanas and wildcats and hunters whose buckshot argued with the exploding seeds of rubber trees.

The Japanese occupation troops established a Kempetai° camp near the factory. The screams from there would have been more horrible if it were not for the thumping engines of the bee hoon factory.

Thiam Soo grew. Two other children were born. The hard-packed earthen floor of the factory was cemented over.

The father installed a boiler, created new machinery, applied his own study method, which our own National Productivity Board° would be proud of, and by Liberation Day° he was employing twelve men at the rate of eight dollars per day.

It is substantially true to say that his accounts, whatever there were of them, would show that he prospered. But all his profits went into the construction and reconstruction of machines.

Today, a similar factory in Jurong employs eighty labourers producing 80,000 katis of bee hoon a month. Thiam Soo's father, with his self-made, handmade machines, produced 45,000 tons in addition to 20,000 tons of laksa with less than one-tenth of the workforce.

The father still wears only black shorts and a smile. His anger—cool, calculating, and terrible—was unleashed at precise and remembered times, for which he is praised. The result of his anger was generally acknowledged as fate or destiny.

As when reported to him that he should have allowed Thiam Soo to run away from home in 1950, instead of chasing him half a mile down the main road and with a coil of rope tying him up and dragging him home, he said: "Maybe it was destiny that my son should burn down this factory of my hands. My son, the man?"

It was at this time that the father asked me to write a reply to a letter from Holland. They wanted to buy his bee hoon in quantity. He expanded his factory, modified his machinery and was in the export business. His song or, as he said it, his whistle, was strong in him.

Thiam Soo was set to work in the factory as a labourer after he had been systematically rejected by three schools for lack of affinity with studies.

He aspired to be owner and sole manager of the factory. "Yes," his father said.

There were thirty people employed in the factory then: a thug, a tiger chief on the run, a few who read the editorials daily in the Chinese papers; the rest were rain watchers because there was no work on a rainy day. They later gravitated towards easier work elsewhere and the father was forced to improve his machines.

Salaries were pegged at eighteen dollars per working day per person, which was generally considered to be a reasonable wage in the mid-fifties.

There was this unnameable serpent coiled in Thiam Soo but it slumbered, dormant. What for a time lost the father his factory, the tabernacle of his life was a purely predictable matter. A general strike°.

Such commotion was never before seen along Upper Thompson Road. A lorry came from party headquarters with banners and collapsible chairs and a large sheet of tarpaulin with which they erected a shelter by the main road under the rubber trees.

Fists were waved at passersby and slogans were shouted and the occasional rock thrown at British soldiers on their way back to camp. It was good fun for the first few days.

The shelter became a rallying point for the children in the neighbourhood and for the girlfriends of the men. But gradually there were fewer and fewer adults to be seen as in twos and threes they sneaked away to hold council with the father.

"I have done you no wrong!" he protested in hurt and anger. "Why do you seek to destroy your rice bowls and my life?" And the wiser among them said: "Uncle, you just do not understand politics."

The factory remained idle for twenty-seven days. The machines and the workers hung about like stray dogs in the sun. They waited for work. Many intermediaries were called upon to plead with the father to set the factory going again. At this time of idleness and apathy, Thiam Soo became an aficionado of the gaming table.

The father, who had withdrawn into himself, like the men about him, felt his fingers ache for work. So he relented. He gathered the workers around him and exerted many promises of loyalty and increased productivity, most of which they kept. Because of the tremendous incentive he devised, he gave gratis an equal division of the factory to each worker, so long as they continued to work alongside him. He kept two shares of the same proportion for himself. He had lost the factory, but the machines throbbed again and all was well.

As it happened, workers gradually left, some to work their vegetable gardens, some to rest their age and others to work in construction gangs for small change.

Then Thiam Soo claimed his inheritance. The father had been continually improving his machines as the work force dwindled, and although he knew his son to be a heavy gambler and brutish in his laziness, he granted the entire bee hoon business to him, plus a van and a telephone. The father on his part ventured into the manufacture of laksa.

But Thiam Soo's gambling debts are heavy. He is also not around to supervise and administer the business. The father, who gave him full autonomy on the control and operation of the plant, cannot witness the destruction of this, his own Tabernacle.

He has devised a new machine, the output of which will dwarf his son's production rate. He will make bee hoon again in his own corner of the factory.

Thiam Soo knows that the chips are down. He has forbidden the father to make bee hoon. His father should not prosper if he himself cannot. The first step as I have related has already been taken. He has doused all available stock of bee hoon with sump oil. And now he says with dreadful determination that he will make an inferno of the factory—with his father inside.

He is a man now and there is no song in him, only cascades of shadow.

Lion City Filled With Panthers°

HOW MANY PANTHERS are there in our midst?

A panther is a glide of black shadow at night, stealing chickens in Singapore and generally frightening the wits out of children and farmers' wives. Reports on sightings lead us to believe that the Lion City has become a lair for panthers where even the holds of ships are used as dens.

The number of sightings reported by ordinary people, whose natures normally prompt them to run away from the scene of an accident because they do not want to get involved, are amazing in their detail and variety. The bogey-cat terrifies them but they can live with the other species of panther, the more vicious one, the vice-ridden one that robs and maims and kills. Sightings of the two-legged panther are rarely reported.

The four-legged panther, unlike the two-legged one, is a predator that will avoid man if it can. Its body is not more than four feet long. Typically it is tawny and marked with black spots, each formed of a group of smaller spots in a ring. But a form also occurs in which the coat is so dark that the spots scarcely show. This is the so-called black panther. They readily climb trees but prefer open country to jungle. They prey on mammals from the size of a pig downwards, and are fond of taking domestic goats, dogs and chickens. The panther of Tanjong Rhu weighed twenty-three kilogrammes.

It is presumed that there is one other marauder at large with a penchant for chickens and the odour of adrenalin from frightened people. It has been very much in the eye of the public, who have been alerted and cautioned. Police come armed with a variety of weapons to the scene of the reported sighting and the people are reassured. There is much cheer and holiday spirit as the forces attempt to hunt down the animal. There is not the tight-lipped silence and averted eyes as when a raid is launched against the panther of the two-legged variety.

Chicken thieves we can bear with. After all, how many chickens are there left in Singapore? There are so many who use the valuable energy and muscle of the police force to prevent the imagined destruction of a few chickens. They readily give in to extortion and threat. Reports are made only after robbery and assault. They witness murder and mayhem in the street and they are discreet as the three proverbial monkeys about it all. They do not see or hear or speak. It is amazing that they do not realise that monkey is the favourite meat of the panther, especially the two-legged one.

The two-legged panther comes in diverse breeds. He comes as a rapist of the bodies and minds of children. He appears in the affable guise of a shopkeeper who short-sells. As the dope peddler, the purveyor of prostitution, the unlicensed moneylender, the secret society hood, the armed robber, the vandal, the corrupt public official. They generate fear and awe among the monkeys who are more concerned over the loss of a few chickens than their lives and property. Police are not called in to apprehend these panthers. On the contrary, the police are avoided.

Perhaps something good can result in the appearances and capture of the four-legged panthers in Singapore. Acting immediately on reports of the whereabouts of the cat, the police have always appeared in minutes.

The blaze of publicity that has always followed describing the happening should reassure any monkey of safety and protection whether he be victim or witness or the instrument that helps prevent crime.

We still want to be called the Lion City? Lions roar and are brave. Panthers glide like shadows in the night. They can be identified by the sound of their cough and spit!

The pattern of the panther can be destroyed! °

RADIN

RADIN AND HIS MOTHER lived in a small attap hut that was very beautiful in the early mornings and at nights when the moon shone like soft silver. There was a chicken coop full of chickens in the small garden, and a little house on the top of a pole with many pigeons in it. There was a well in the garden too, and Radin's mother washed the clothes of many people as she stooped beside the well every morning.

Radin swept the garden every day. And he carried water out of the well with a pail for his mother. Radin loved his mother very much and his mother loved him too, although she scolded him when he was naughty.

Kassim was Radin's good friend. He lived near Mu-Lan, who was also Radin's friend. She became his friend when a boy called Ah Tee threw a stone at her, making her cry, and Radin, who was passing by, punched Ah Tee and chased him away.

One day Mu-Lan asked Radin to catch her a little fish that she could rear in a small aquarium by her bedside. Radin said that he would not catch just one fish for her. "No," he said, "I will catch a million fishes for you!" And straight away he ran back home for his rattan ponkis° and then to Kassim's house.

"Come along, Kassim," he shouted, "come and help me catch a million fishes for Mu-Lan!"

Far away from Radin's house, there were many rubber trees, and behind the rubber trees where nobody could see, there was a large place with high lalang and many streams full of shallow clean water and fishes.

Radin and Kassim went to this place. They jumped into the stream, rolling up their trousers so as not to wet them. The water was very cold and there were sudden, faster-than-grasshopper movements as fishes swam away to hide under weeds and rocks. Kassim was upstream, and from that he slowly walked towards Radin, who was holding the ponkis in the water, ready to scoop up any fish swimming away from Kassim.

They stayed in the stream for a long time without catching a single fish. I do not say that Radin and Kassim did not know how to catch a fish. It was not their fault; it was the fault of the ponkis, which was full of large holes, so that every time Radin caught a fish, it just slipped through a hole in the ponkis and swam happily away.

After a very long time, Radin scooped up a wriggling black fish and pressed his hand quickly over it so that it could not escape. Kassim rushed away and came back with a small tin full of water. Radin popped the fish into it and both of them put their heads close looking at the fish swimming around in the tin.

"It's a fighting fish," Kassim whispered, "a champion fighting fish!"

"I'm sure it will beat Ah Tee's fish anyday," Radin said. "Just look at its scales, like a million jewels, blue and green and red and purple …this fish will beat Ah Tee's fish and all the fishes in the world."

Both of them respected the fish very much. It was beautiful and brave. They hurried home, through the rubber trees and over the road, being careful not to shake the water in the tin because that would have made the fish giddy and sick.

"We have to feed this fish and train it to be fierce and clever," Radin said.

Kassim, who remembered many things, said, "What about Mu-Lan? Aren't you going to give her the fish as you promised?"

"Later on, maybe," Radin answered.

Late in the evening, Mu-Lan went to Radin's garden gate and called for him. Radin appeared slowly from behind the house and looked at her.

"Have you caught a fish for me?" Mu-Lan asked.

"No," Radin lied. "I'm doing some work for my mother. I'll catch one for you tomorrow."

Mu-Lan walked away thinking what a good boy Radin was. And Radin went back behind the house and squatted beside Kassim to watch the fighting fish in a bottle, tightly coiling and darting, attacking its own image in a small mirror, its gills opened fiercely, its tail like a small coloured fan, and its body sprinkled with jewels that flashed like a million stars.

"If I gave Mu-Lan this fish," Radin said to Kassim, "she would not know what to do with it. But if we keep it, we can train it to be the champion of the world and sell it for a hundred dollars.

Then I can buy Mu-Lan many lovely presents."

Then Radin's mother, who had been in the kitchen all the time where she could hear them speaking, came out and chased Kassim home and scolded Radin. "You bad boy!" she said. "You broke a promise and told a lie. Now you take this fish straight to Mu-Lan's house. Tell her that you're sorry, give the fish to her, and come back."

Radin felt very ashamed of himself. He picked up the bottle with the fish and walked slowly, with his eyes staring at the ground so that nobody could see how naughty he had been.

Mu-Lan was in her garden and she felt happy when she saw Radin carrying the fish in the bottle.

"I brought the fish to you," Radin said still looking at the ground. "My mother told me to tell you that I'm sorry for telling you a lie." He felt so ashamed that he wished he had never been born.

"Why, it's a fighting fish!" Mu-Lan said. "A beautiful, beautiful fighting fish." And she felt so happy, half-laughing and half-crying. She grew quiet for a little while and then said, "What shall I do now, Radin? I don't know how to train this fish. Will you train it for me, Radin?"

He shouted, "Yes!" feeling suddenly as happy as she was. He grabbed the bottle from her and ran back home where he told his mother all that had happened.

"See, Radin," his mother said, "by being honest you not only have the fighting fish, but you've also made Mu-Lan happy." And Radin knew that what his mother said was very true. His mother was always right.

THE OPEN AIR MARKET

THERE ARE THOSE who may say that I love the Open Air Market in Kuching, Sarawak, because of a mother and child I saw there lovelier than a Madonna and child by Murillo°. But that is not true. I love the place without knowing exactly why.

It is a long shed with a strong roof, and eating stalls and tables spilling into a triangular space shaped by three roads. It is the only place in Kuching that remains open right through the night.

Business begins with a drumbeat from the mosque nearby, and a prayer amplified by loudspeakers. A prayer as unrestrained in emotion as a Spanish flamenco song.

The shed housing the market is lit by dusty fluorescent lights stuck to the rafters and hissing pressure lamps like low stars everywhere. There are nine stalls run by Malays—their golden green bananas bunched on hooks and noodles frying with chilli and sauce. One stall belongs to an Indian and fourteen to Chinese and fifty more fanning out to the road. About three hundred people come here every night and they feel, without noticing, the hum of whispers and talk and strong laughter and hawkers shouting. The steam and smell of food, frying and boiling. The scavenging dogs and little boys selling sheaves of lottery tickets and the tinkle of chopsticks on porcelain. A child bathes under a standpipe and a billiards room across the road with enamelled balls clicks like slow castanets. Shuffling, sad-eyed beggars wander around here and a man from Nepal sells coloured beads and stones; this man says that he once saw God on a green hill in Siam.

There is much life in this place and people come here to be absorbed and comforted by it.

The hawkers who run the market sell an average of fifteen pounds of meat every night plus twenty pounds of rice, using eleven pounds of vegetable oil and forty-five pounds of charcoal to prepare colourful, tasty dishes in six minutes flat. Meat stalls close down by one in the morning, except for the odd ones selling coffee and cakes. At this time there are still twenty people sitting in the open, most of whom will be here till morning. No one talks and small noises are magnified, but the strong feeling of life never leaves the market. Policemen walk slowly on duty and dogs scrounge freely and a beggar writes on scraps of paper and throws them like small white flags into the drain.

The lights on the roof beams of the shed dissolve into the colour of night and long shadows suddenly shoot in between the closed stalls. The lights come on again at four in the morning when the wooden clogs on fast feet of early hawkers sound sharply on cement as two dry bamboos stuck together. In a few minutes there is hot pork gruel for fishermen who leave at five in the morning in their boats, through the mist over the deep river to the sea. Now the Kuching Municipal Council trucks rumble forward sweeping the streets with their mechanical brushes, and a thousand starlings shriek with high small voices over the heads of a small crowd waiting for breakfast in the blueness of just before dawn, when again a prayer floats out from the loudspeakers of the mosque.

Mei-Lin [B]

I.

IN THE MARKETPLACE in the pearl of the dawn, before the red blood of the sun veined the sky, Mei-Lin, with ribbons in her hair and her baby doll peeping warmly from under her blouse, examined her province.

The thatched roof stretched acres over cement floors that were never clean of odour, because of the meat smells and the never-dissipating human smells and especially the fish and prawn and squid smells, hovering five feet over the floor area.

In ten minutes' time, trucks laden with greens would appear together with the first stall-holders, with fingers like teeth waiting to crunch, and in an orgy of satisfaction display the vegetables.

Meat would arrive later, the pick-up wagon coming with the night catch of fish from kelongs° and nets and lines. Kerosene sloshed in pressure lamps as they were lighted above tiled trestles upon which fish were flung like streams of pearl fire. They were fresh and fine-scaled; some of them arched their bodies and flung their tails. They smelled clean enough to taste on the tongue.

When the sun pervaded the pearl of the dawn, the malodorous quality of the market would appear together with the yellow of baskets, the colour of sarongs and a peep of thighs from high-slit cheongsams. Husbands would be rare. There would be a proliferation of small boys, but Mei-Lin was not allowed to associate with or even speak to them. Their arguing and fighting were influenced by descriptions of Chinese martial arts, which they gleaned from motion pictures they viewed for twenty cents per show at the open-air theatre at night by the marketplace, and preceded their normal ambitions. They sold guppies, black mollies°, goldfish and Mexican swordtails° in basins, and worms for fish. The open-air entrance displayed posters and glossy photographs of whatever pugilistic spectaculars from Shaw Brothers° were popular at that time.

Mei-Lin approached her favourite place on the lane that bisected the theatre and the eating stalls where the old man was to come. The folding table, the stool, the joss sticks against the brass idol, and the slips of blood-red paper had been set.

When the old bent man in rusty black clothes whose stall it was arrived, Mei-Lin, who never feared him, paid deference by hiding in the shadow of the pork-sellers stall. The old man had fingernails eleven inches long from the flesh of the fingers, like grey centipedes suddenly alive when light and air pervade the rock under which they lie. The nail of his forefinger, however, was cut close to enable him to write predictions on the slips of red paper.

He saw Mei-Lin, this wise old prophet who foolishly thought that he was a charlatan. He had been here only one year after having fled from Ipoh° where he was born, raised and taught his practice because he had preferred to listen to the advice of those who believed that alchemy and prophecy was a trade instead of a murmur of the soul.

The market, Mei-Lin's province, was in order. So was the order of her life.

Then, from the closed attap wings lying over her house beside the market came the breath of a boiling light and the vulgar roar of her name from her mother, puffy-lidded and with dirt in her eyes, to come home.

Mei-Lin consoled the doll on her arm and ran, shouting, "I'm coming, I'm coming!"

II.

Madam Chan—her voice rancorous as the cock in the vicinity urging the advent of the sun, as if without their crow there would be no morning, descendants of that supreme con-artist Orpheus° and to hell with the role of Eurydice in the matter—was extremely upset.

Johnny, her son-in-law, lived in his luxury apartment on Orchard Road near the hotel he worked in. Johnny Tan! Tan, instead of her family name Chan! What sin against tradition! A crime against the ancestors of the honourable family of Koh, whose yellow, framed photographs peered solemnly from the walls of the teak-paralleled rooms of the attap house, a mansion that once had been an earth-floor hovel. Johnny Tan, who had seduced her daughter Swee Lay, raped her mind to marry into another clan, had given her the name Anna. What blasphemy! And Swee Lay, having been disowned and only recently returned to grace was quite complacent and content. The fortune teller had said that it was difficult to see if something good would come of the match.

Her husband's ashes rested in the urn on the altar, and his spirit appeared to have lost all interest, despite her supplication prayers and joss sticks and food and fruit and wine offerings, in the matter of her concern. It appeared that the bastard condoned this disgrace to the family. And Johnny had phoned a moment ago to say that Anna, no, Swee Lay, wanted Mei-Lin to spend the weekend with them. And oh! Hosts of Heaven, Johnny treated Mei-Lin as if she were grown and of a marriageable capacity. And Mei-Lin only nine!

Madam Chan had reminded Johnny that his every address to her was an insult to her dignity and her ancestors and slammed the phone down feeling highly satisfied. But when Swee Lay, her favourite but erring daughter, called to repeat the request, she was faced with losing the insidious control that she had over her, the insinuations of creed and custom, the hold of tradition and the clawing legs of determination of cause and effect, of shattering clan taboos in every circumstance.

Madam Chan agreed to release Mei-Lin to the home of Johnny for one night and offered joss sticks to the household god that she would see her safe again and innocent, with pigtails and ribbons from the man whom she despised and held in suspect.

She called Mei-Lin's name again. Her daughter came out of the pearl light of dawn and said, "Yes, Mother?" With her curls and ribbons and laughter and her doll. As the sun clawed up into the sky.

THE MOMENT OF TRUTH

IN THE EVENING, after the funeral, there was a drizzle of rain and the smell of dissolved clay, and the men who had joined the procession to the grave sat in the coffee shop in the kampung.

They were gambling men—a breed not given to much talk—prone to drinking and fighting. They did not gamble on the turn of card or dice, but on the quick courage of fighting cocks and fish and spiders.

There was a pit in the vacant lot in the back of the coffee shop where fighting cocks were matched; fat glass jars with fighting fish inside were lined in tiers along one wall of the shop; fierce spiders were kept in tins, tight in men's pockets. But the boy would no longer be there to see men's desperate contests for life, or to share in the tense moments of reckoning, the prayers mouthed but never uttered, the shouted curses, the full-bodied exultations of victory. Kassim was dead!

A river slid through a rubber estate away from the kampung, and in a pool where three streams met, clear water coursed a few inches over deep grey mud. A rubber tapper had passed by there that morning and noticed two pale feet sticking out of the mud. A grave was dug that same afternoon, and the boy buried.

Bottles of beer were opened and served in the coffee shop. A bottle of whiskey appeared and was passed around. The fighting fish dozed lazily in their separate jars. A match had not been suggested. The men drank slowly out of their mugs of beer laced with whisky. Then, unable to contain himself, one of them shouted, "Ah hell! Why did the damn fool kill himself? He was only sixteen."

"Why? Because his whole life was involved in a total passion for courage. He worshipped courage." It was an old man who spoke, a thin, brown old man, shrunken but not wrinkled, his face deeply creased with lines of rich experience and wisdom. He had fought in wars and sailed across the seas. He had been a professional boxer for a short time and, until a few years before, a wholly satisfying lover to many women. The old man had also been the boy's idol and best friend.

—

I was with him last night, the old man said. We talked in his room. His face was grey and there was the look of shame in his eyes. "Pa-Chi," he said, "I…I stole Montezuma." You know, of course, that Montezuma is the name of my fighting cock, which was missing for the past week.

"Why did you do it, Kassim?" I asked him.

"I was afraid and I needed his courage," he told me.

"Well, since you required his assistance," I said, "I shall consider that you borrowed Montezuma. The question of theft does not arise. So there is no need to fear for your honour." But my attitude did nothing to help the boy. His face turned paler and I saw tears well up in his eyes. He was trying desperately to control himself.

"Montezuma was the bravest thing I ever saw," he said. "I cooked him last night and ate him."

What was I to say? I have already saved twenty-six dollars, and I need only two dollars more for a deck passage to Sarawak. It had been my intention to take Montezuma to the cockfighting pits there and find my fortune. It is not good to be an old man without money.

A large tear rolled down Kassim's cheek. I was embarrassed for him. I looked around his room and saw steel daggers and kris arranged on one wall. There were sharp bamboo spears that he had fashioned himself on another wall. Across the room, thousands of storybooks reaching up to the ceiling. The fourth wall was bare except for a picture torn from a magazine, a colourful photo of a black fighting bull, its horns tossed high, blood dripping from shoulder to hoof. I remembered that the boy had once told me that his greatest desire was to be a matador, to stand alone, dressed in a suit of lights in a bull ring, with only a scarlet cape in his hands, to hear the snarl of drum and high trumpet call and to execute graceful patterns with the cape, working a maddened bull so close to his body as to feel its sharp horns grazing his side, the crowd shouting deliriously, "Olé! Olé!" as, with each swirl of his cape, they recognised him as being of pure courage.

With my eyes fixed on the picture, I repeated to him what he had told me before. I told him that I would acquire another fighting cock and still make that trip to Sarawak. Passionately, I said that the future was a kingdom I would make. I invited him to share this adventure with me. I would name my new fighting cock Conquistador.

But even these things failed to comfort the boy. I begged him to tell me the whole reason for his behaviour, and he said, "I don't think you would understand, Pa-Chi. You have never felt fear scurrying like long-legged spiders across your heart every waking moment of the day, feeling frightened always and not knowing why. I am a coward, Pa-Chi, I found out today."

I know you are surprised. I also was surprised when Kassim said that to me. Hadn't we always considered him to be the bravest young man we'd ever met? Didn't he prove himself time and time again, more times than necessary, in fact? We have all felt the cold fingers of fear, but why did he call himself a coward? I asked him, of course, and he told me and that is why I say that he actually worshipped courage, a mystical concept of courage. Consider now, the reason for his statement—and this I believe must also be the reason for his death.

—

The old man paused to drink deeply from his mug of beer laced with the tang of whiskey (and consequently very satisfying). The lights in the coffee shop gleamed brighter. The darkness of night had softly enveloped the kampung a moment before. This was the time of the December monsoon and the steady patter of drizzle had changed to sharp needles of rain, misting the night and chattering in whispery gusts upon the roof of the coffee shop. The gamblers listened to the old man without interruption or comment.

The old man lit a cigar, puffed at it, and looked at the gamblers to gauge the intensity of their concentration.

—

Kassim told me, the old man continued, of the situation of his mother and father. You know his mother, a very exciting woman; I think some of you know her all too well. His father loves drink above all, and his happiness after drink is beating the woman. Kassim grew up in this kind of house. He related details, which, out of respect to his mother and father, I do not care to repeat; but they were sad and terrible things. Kassim had also been in love for some years with a girl who did not know of his existence. His love for her was a terrible ecstasy, so intense that he dared not approach her for fear that he would not be paid in like value. That is why he was always with us watching the razored cocks stab and rip at each other, witnessing the flaring of gills and fins and tails of fighting fish and the jewel points glittering on their tight bodies, and seeing the calculated parrying and thrust and kill of our spiders. Kassim was with us because he was troubled and in love. These things may have left an ever-present coldness in his heart, he may have longed for the sleep of death for those reasons, but a final, sharp barb was necessary to demand his life.

This barb, this excuse if you like, was presented to him on a Tuesday morning, the day before I allowed you to examine the qualities of Montezuma. It was at the hour before dawn, and Kassim went to the field between our kampung and the rubber estate, to exercise. He did this every morning to encourage discipline and strength. Ropes of mist hung over the field as Kassim shadowboxed, and, standing stiffly, practiced with an imaginary cape for the bullfights of Madrid and Mexico. When he paused to rest and to feel the breeze picking off droplets of perspiration with cool hands, he saw someone walk slowly out of the mist towards him. A boy of the same height and build as Kassim, dressed like Hang Tuah° with headdress and sarong belted around his waist and a kris in the folds of his sarong. Kassim felt a wave of fear overwhelm him as he realised he had to fight this other boy, as one animal does battle with another to defend its lair or hunting ground.

The boy strode up to Kassim and faced him. His lips curled in a sneer of contempt. He raised his hand deliberately and slapped Kassim across the face. He stepped back and waited for Kassim to return the blow, but Kassim's arms and legs had grown soft and his heart shivered as if it would burst out of his body. Kassim was afraid to fight, and the boy dressed like Hang Tuah, recognising Kassim's fear, laughed out loud. Kassim's shame was great. He lowered his eyes, feeling the flutter of his heart and the weakness of his limbs. When he raised his eyes again, he saw the other boy striding through the mist until it closed over him and blocked him from view.

And now, Kassim felt his strength returning and also an increase of shame so acute that he felt like crying. The moment of truth that he'd longed for had come to him—and he'd been found wanting in courage.

Kassim walked slowly home and to bed. He lay in bed the whole day. He did not even get up to eat. These things he told me. We did not see him for a number of days, remember?

Kassim lay in bed until the hour of dawn on the following morning. He was filled with resolve and courage. He had rehearsed in his mind exactly how he would defeat the boy dressed like Hang Tuah. He had starved himself to intensify his sense of purpose. He had meditated on the strength of his body until it now sang like a lethal weapon. But he was still possessed by a touch of doubt over which he had no control.

He drew a pail of water from the well in his garden, washed his face and drank enough of it to wash the dryness from his mouth. Then, groping in the darkness under a bush, he withdrew a bottle in which he kept his favourite fighting fish. He upended the bottle on his palm and drained off water until the glistening fish wriggled in his hand. He looked at it a moment, thinking of its courage, then swiftly he swallowed it. And the little touch of doubt in him seemed to vanish.

With confidence now, Kassim went to the field where he always exercised. And there, at the same instant as the morning before, the boy dressed like Hang Tuah appeared through the ropes of mist. Again, Kassim felt his strength drain away from him as his cowardice made itself clear. With head hung low, he waited for the other boy to slap him. He was punched in the stomach instead and collapsed in a flood of pain.

When he recovered, the boy dressed like Hang Tuah had vanished through the mist.

Kassim stole Montezuma later that morning. With my fighting cock, he cooked a rich stew and finished the whole thing himself. Then he summoned me to his room to confess his guilt and to tell me all that I have told you.

I think that on the field before dawn this morning, he faced his opponent for the last time and found that even Montezuma could not restore his courage. I'm sure that the boy dressed like Hang Tuah must have degraded and shamed him. Afterwards, walking in despair, Kassim reached the pool in the rubber estate, faced his final, terrible moment of truth, and plunged headlong into the mud to seek his salvation.

—

The gamblers in the coffee shop breathed out a sigh, and with a touch of water in their eyes, reached for their drinks. Was it possible that all of what the old man had related could be true? There was the part about the boy dressed like Hang Tuah. Who was he? No boy of that description lived in their kampung or in any other kampung that they knew of.

"Did I not tell you that Kassim actually worshipped courage?" the old man said. "Maybe the other boy was the god of courage come down from his fortress, to bring to his subject Kassim the honour of the Moment of Truth. And he found Kassim unprepared."

MY SAY

I ASSURE YOU by the bones of the saints that I have tried to be a father to admire and emulate. A good man. A man of composure, gruff but gentle, a little distant perhaps and yet a father who handles children with delicacy and fine understanding. A consistent man having reached a stage of harmony and compatibility with his children.

Therefore, I can only conclude that when I smacked the backside of my daughter Jacinta, it must have been purely a matter of quick reflexes on my part. I fell off her bicycle whilst demonstrating the finer points of equilibrium and she laughed. So I deflated her ego.

Mark you, this is the child to whom I wrote eleven years ago when she was one year old. I imagined that she would emerge from her cocoon a ballerina by Degas°, with the charm and scintillation of Copland's El Salón México°, a lotus petal no less. And I with quiet pride would escort her to places of marvel and sophistication. Now, the less said about what I secretly cherished the better. After finishing with the girl guides and having pounded the piano to pieces (in what she fondly imagines is practising), she will probably join the Armed Forces.

But when she was still in her cot with dimpled wrists and knees, placing my movements with adoring eyes, I addressed her as follows:

"You will, I know, one day charge me with allegations of irresponsibility. You will do so kindly of course, with much tact and kindness and great affection. You will say that I should have given you some positive advice on life and happiness. Then I shall smile happily and produce these words which I write you on your first birthday.

"Well Jacinta, little flower of my heart, it is necessary to remember that you must always be free to preserve all the rules or break them if you have to. Feel as exhilaratingly free as the pup I saw this morning racing crazily along the seashore, lime-sweet spray and the early sun matted on his coat. Do not forget that life is a story told by God to each one of us. Only a story. A story that we personally see and feel. Sad and happy stories of pain and courage and sacrifice, of bitterness and despair, joy and love. Stories we actually live through, with God as the master storyteller imparting a different take to every single one of us, with birth as its beginning and what we call death as its end.

"And we are free to hear the story out or to run away like bored and restless little children. Of course, those who run away discover it is impossible to find their way back to the lap of God when the story has been told. So, Jacinta, use your freedom wisely…"°

I gave her this piece of yellowing paper after the incident of the bicycle lesson but she had other things on her mind (at least when she sat on it). Being the considerate father that I am, believing in the delegation and division of responsibility, I handed her over to her mother—who, ten years ago, contemplated divorcing me—for further instruction.

The affair of the near-divorce was precipitated by my son, Zero. Yes, Zero. If we had had another girl, she would by common consent have been Francesca Bella. But I was quite clear in my mind that a boy would be nothing other than Zero. Think of it, he can never be less than zero! His is a natural platform for achievement. Every mark scored in school, every act in his life cannot but be a logical advancement. And if his first initial appears on his test paper as well, he does not own the copyright to it, does he?

At the baptismal font, however, the godparents begged to decline the signal honour that I had bestowed upon them. The priest, upon learning of the infant's intended name, did a most unpriestly thing. He called me aside and in a very grave whisper, threatened to assault me. And so my son was christened Geraldo Mario, and there was a sound like leaves soughing in the breeze. It was a concerted sigh from those assembled in church. There was much merriment and relief after the baptism and the wine gurgled sweetly down many throats. But there were some in the house who looked disconcertedly at my happiness. It was generally postulated that I had overcome the folly of my thoughts, that I had forgotten the magic name, Zero!

But I had learnt how to play poker during quiet nights in Sarawak, and my teachers were masters of the art. I still held the trump card: my son's birth had yet to be registered. So on the very last day permissible, I presented myself at the Registry of Births and with deep pride and dignity announced my son's name: ZERO Geraldo Mario Nalpon. I will never forget the fineness, the solemnity of that moment. I had named my son. Many friends who doubted my courage in naming my son threw a small feast in repayment of a wager.

The courage that they failed to recognise was to surface in that moment of truth, when I delivered the mint-new birth certificate into my wife's keeping. She was too busy consulting her lawyer to notice the exhibition of my courage. Neither did I, for that matter.

Well, Zero is getting along fine in school. He's had his share of fights to stamp out ridicule and in Art class he signs his name proudly, ZERO.

He's a good student and a good scout. He loves adventure as much as I do—the hikes and the camping, the fishing and a bit of shooting, well-watered whisky to keep out the chill at night and an appreciation of feminine charms. He can safely aspire to be a smuggler or just a contented bum if he succeeds in traversing the age of puberty.

I have given Jacinta her sermon and Zero his name. I am content in the knowledge that I have done my duty. I too must now rest.

THE WAYANG AT
EIGHT MILESTONE°

KIM LAY MET TONY at the Changi bus terminus°. They had just killed a man that night. A group of them had ambushed the man in a coffee shop; Kim Lay had stabbed him and Tony had gouged his eyes out. The man was supposed to have murdered Kim Lay's younger brother, Tony's best friend, by a knife thrust through the eye into the brain.

It wasn't until later when they found out that they had killed the wrong man.

Tony sat in the bus shed, his head hanging low. His pocket was wet with pale red blood and he fondled the round soft thing in his pocket. He heard footsteps and looked up.

"You took a long time," he said slowly. His eyes were very red and his mouth was caught in the snarl that had appeared on his lips at the time of the murder.

"The police caught Johnny," Kim Lay said. "The swine told

them our names. We've got to get the hell out of here!"

Tony looked at him dully. He saw that Kim Lay's eyes were big and soft and red and Tony could see the trailing things behind them. The two men got onto a bus and sat at the back. Tony saw that all the other people in the bus had big round eyes perched under their foreheads; round, wet, red eyes with slimy nerve strands attached to them.

Kim Lay looked at Tony and, seeing his eyes, knew what was in his mind. "Look out of the window," he said quietly. Tony remained staring at the other passengers as if hypnotised. Kim Lay grabbed a fistful of Tony's hair and with his other hand he forced Tony's face towards the window. Tony saw the blue street lights and saw red, wet eyeballs in them. And his long, strong fingers, which had probed into eye sockets, now played with the soft shape in his pocket. Looking out of the window, his face was locked stiffly by eyes fixed onto the street lights.

The bus started and ran fast, leaning round corners, screeching at the wheels. It roared four miles along lighted roads and four more along narrow, winding roads, and the moon dodged between tree tops and sped in crazy slants across the sky as the bus careened around corners and finally down a slope and shuddered to a halt.

"Down here," Kim Lay said. Tony followed dumbly. Most of the passengers were getting off the bus; many more were crowding outside to get in.

The night sky was black. Not the clear, clean black of space, but black like furry velvet lightly sprinkled with powder and rubbed in. There were no stars, no clouds. The shadow of the earth had eaten away one quarter of the moon, the big, horrid, yellow moon defusing light that melted into the sky like a smear of margarine on a slice of burnt toast.

The wayang° was being performed on the outskirts of a graveyard in honour of the dead, on top of a bare hill of dried red clay and patches of withered grass. Some of the crowd packed tight close to the stage, or stood on tombstones, not minding the bones of the dead beneath the soil. There was double row of hawker stalls along the slope with hissing, crackling oil in pans and mee being fried, and flutes and drums spread out on canvas, and fashionable spectacles with powerless lenses sold at two dollars each. This wayang troupe was well known, and it performed to perfection; the expensive costumes of the players glimmered and glittered, the rich colours burning through the eyes and into the mind. Heavy makeup and exaggerated beards and gestures and costumes of old China and stage scenery, and all the while, the screeching whine of fiddles and smashing of thin cymbals and gongs and tock-tocking on wood and the movements on stage.

Kim Lay had to guide Tony up the hill through the crowd, the heat, the burning colours and the noise. Tony felt their eyes on him, hundreds of them, all big, round, red and wet. And with soft trailing things behind their eyes.

A dirty white hen scratched in the grass beside the red clay path. It was a crazy old hen; everybody living in that area knew about it. It slept in the daytime and scratched around at night. It liked streets and people and noise. The feathers of the hen poked out in all directions as if it had been plucked clean and the feathers pasted back randomly, like a badly stuffed feather pillow, and some parts were quite bare, showing pink, pimply skin. For seven years it hadn't laid a single egg; two weeks ago, it began crowing like a young rooster, and a week ago, it stopped crowing and laid an egg, a small warm irregular ball with a soft skin. Since it had laid the egg, it never slept in the night. Kim Lay kicked it as he and Tony walked by.

In a corner of the cemetery, in the long shadow of a tombstone, a balding Chinese fortune-teller ran his business; a spitting white flame of a carbide lamp lit him in parts. His face was like the knotted bark of an old rubber tree, hardened and spotted with white light and black darkness. It was, in a way, a simple face, a few grey hairs on his upper lip and chin, and a body hunched and muscled with age. His head was bent and his body was still. He constantly referred to a large, thin, paper-bound volume crammed with Chinese characters and coloured pictures, marking it now and then, adding new characters like fantastic black spiders, his ballpoint pen flowing smoothly over the crisp, yellowing pages.

Kim Lay guided Tony away from the path and walked over the grass to where the fortune-teller sat in the shadow of the tombstone.

A greasy and dirt-hardened square of green tarpaulin was stretched out in front of him, covering the lumps and bumps and hollows of the earth. A many-sided disk, cut out of a piece of wood and painted, lay in the middle of the canvas, and two more pieces of wood, with the same number of sides, were placed one on top of another, above the bottom one. In the middle of the tray stood a small thistle-shaped, sand-filled porcelain urn. Joss sticks, yellow on red stems, were stuck into the sand, fuming fragrant white smoke.

Kim Lay and Tony squatted down beside the fortune-teller. He did not look up. His body was still. His hands closed the book he was writing on. He put away his pen.

Red cards, that were actually slim, flat books, were placed in a circle around the urn, overlapping each other. The fortune-teller would pick up one of these cards after referring to the big book, open it, and read the fortunes from the gaudy illustrations and characters, now old and slightly faded with sweat and use and age. In the shadow of the quiet tombstone that seemed to possess life, but not wanting anyone to know of the living soul deep in the stone, lay pictures of dragons with gleaming green scales, black snakes with lolling red tongues, and leaping yellow tigers and demons.

The fortune-teller pointed to the circle of cards. Kim Lay stretched out his hand and pulled one away from the circle. The fortune-teller picked it up. He opened the card and held it up to the light. A black, stiffly coiling snake with a flicking forked tongue was imprinted on it. He closed it and put it back and Kim Lay felt the beating of his heart because of the bad omen.

Kim Lay drew another card from the circle. It was opened to show a similar snake. He tried another card and saw another black snake and he felt the sting of the snake in his mind.

He took out thirty cents from his pocket and threw it on the canvas. When he rose and led Tony away, the fortune-teller reached out for the money and flung it far over the dark tombstones.

Kim Lay led Tony to one of the stalls and bought a big, brass-handled switchblade. He looked around him and smelt and felt the heat and the sounds and life in the air. The fortune-teller in the shadow of the tombstone saw him clutch the knife and walk with Tony across the grass, over the overgrown parts of the cemetery, towards the darkness of the high bamboo on the hill.

The crazy white hen trotted behind them, leaving a trail of dirty white feathers in the long grass.

On this night, a boy also wandered the wayang in the Chinese cemetery. He did not notice the crowds, the noise, the heat. He saw around the corners and in far places—the far quiet places where carbide lights hissed bright and the people did not make much money. The boy stumbled along to these places and smiled at the grim-faced men with sad eyes who sold flutes. He then stooped down and picked up a flute and played, searching for a melody that he had never known, until the sad eyes of the men softened and their mouths relaxed to easy smiles that had taken long, long days to reach down the short space between the mind and the mouth. The boy gently put the carved flute back in the pile, looking at the men regretfully because he wished with all his heart that he could have a bamboo flute to play in the evenings.

The boy walked up the crooked clay path and saw, a ways to the left of him, a little point of light among the tombstones. He walked over the stubby grass to the fortune-teller and smiled a greeting to him. Then he walked up the hill to the high bamboo, watching where he placed his feet because it was easy to fall among the stones and holes carpeted by bamboo blades. Then he heard a clucking and scratching through the darkness near where three stunted pineapple plants grew. The boy stopped and wondered about the sound, and slowly moved with his shadow trailing behind him to where the crazy white hen clucked and grumbled as it pecked little red ants away from the empty eye sockets of Tony.

There was plenty of blood on the ground, and brown and thick on Tony's face and around his mouth, snarling even in death. Kim Lay knelt tightly near Tony with his face to the ground and his hands gripping a knife that was twisted in his stomach, high up under the bridge of his chest.

The boy hurried away from the bamboo, feeling the taste of bile in his mouth. And he let all his feelings run away and lock themselves somewhere secret, so that he could pretend that the whole thing had been a nasty dream.

NOTES

Arb.	Arabic
b.m.	Bahasa Melayu (Malay)
aut.	Autobiographical notes
d. cant.	Cantonese
d. hind.	Hindi
d. hokk.	Hokkien
Ind.	Indonesian
unk.	Origin unknown

Mei-Lin

kramat or keramat [*b.m.*]: Muslim grave of or shrine for a holy man; in Malay tradition, keramats are often haunted

on tick: old British term for credit at a small shop or bar

dived for corals [*aut.*]: Nalpon, an expert swimmer and diver, often went coral diving and swimming in the quarries and coasts of Pulau Ubin and other islands.

mountain dew: euphemism for whiskey

ghost stories [*aut.*]: Many of Nalpon's own stories are ostensibly ghost stories; see "The Appointment", "The Mango Tree" and "A Soul for Anna Lim"

The Rose and the Silver Key

Dhoby Ghaut [*d. hind.*]: washing or laundry place, an urban area in central Singapore; in colonial times a place where Indian laundrymen washed and dried clothes

sarabat [*unk.*]: a hot drink made of ginger and water

sarabat stall: Hamid's stall appears to be positioned directly opposite the Cathay Theatre, a popular local cinema

betel nut or paan: an addictive preparation of areca nut, slaked lime and often, tobacco, wrapped in betel leaf; chewers often have stained red teeth

gangsters: criminal gangs frequently demanded protection money from local stall holders in the 1950s and 1960s

Tony Curtis hairstyle: ducktail hairstyle of a 1950s American actor, later made famous by Elvis Presley

thirsty schoolboy [*aut.*]: Nalpon, went to the nearby St Joseph's Institution and frequented coffee shops and stalls in this area in the late 1950s

Cathay Theatre [*aut.*]: built in 1939, the Cathay was a principal cinema in Singapore during the 1950s and 1960s; Nalpon was a regular patron

all the money he had: possibly a reference to Jesus' remark on the poor widow who "gave all she had" (Mark 12: 41-44)

Mahsuri

Nalpon's version of this legend differs significantly from the local, traditional legend.

Kedah: Northwestern Malay state adjacent to the Thai border

Tungku Abdul Rahman: Chief Minister of the Federation of Malaya from 1955, and the country's first Prime Minister from independence in 1957 until 1970; he remained Prime Minister after Sabah, Sarawak, and Singapore joined the federation in 1963, forming Malaysia

A Soul for Anna Lim

samshu [*d. cant.*]: a distilled spirit made from fermented rice or coconut; Nalpon frequented samshu shops in Little India with his friends; by the 1980s, most samshu shops had disappeared

decline and fall: a playful allusion to Edward Gibbon's The History of the Decline and fall of the Roman Empire (1776-89)

4-digit lottery: 4-digits or 4-D, a popular lottery since its introduction in Singapore by the Turf Club in May 1966

five-foot way: a covered area sheltering the pavement in front of a traditional shophouse

Timepieces

Kandang Kerbau Hospital [*b.m.*]: "buffalo shed"; established as a small general hospital in 1858, it is the largest hospital specialising in healthcare for women and children in Singapore; now known as KK Women's and Children's Hospital

Stamford Canal: now culverted canal running east, almost parallel to Orchard Road, from Cuscaden Road to the Kallang Basin, now Marina Reservoir

Indonesian agent: according to some accounts, the racial riots of September 1964 that errupted in the kampungs of Singapore were instigated by Indonesian agents

Impressions of Island Life

hollow wooden log: traditional Malay method of calling Muslim worshippers to congregational prayer

koleh [*b.m.*]: fishing boat

rojak [*b.m.*]: a traditional fruit and vegetable salad dish commonly found in Indonesia, Malaysia and Singapore; in Malaysia and Singapore, the term 'rojak' is also used as a colloquial expression for an eclectic mix, often to describe the multi-ethnic character of Malaysian and Singaporean society

Trengganu: a coastal state in the north east of Malaysia

government's floating dispensary: mobile means of bringing modern medicine to the small communities inhabiting the islands around Singapore (see "New Floating Dispensary for Islands", *Straits Times*, 19 January 1951)

bidan [*b.m.*]: midwife

ten miles from Singapore: this detail suggests that the two islands Nalpon refers to are Pulau Pawai and Pulau Sudong (which was renowned for its coral reef and would have attracted Nalpon) (see "Pulau Pawai Men Say: No Ghosts", *Straits Times*, 20 August 1950)

The Spirit of the Moon

Iblis [*Arb.*] or Shaitan: the Islamic name for the devil or Satan

four angels: not part of Muslim Orthodox belief; Nalpon's description resembles traditional Christian animal iconography of the winged man, lion, bull and eagle representing the four evangelists, Matthew, Mark, Luke and John respectively; the tiger, replacing the lion, helps give the symbolism a Southeast Asian resonance

Gibra'il or Jibreel [*Arb.*]: the Islamic name for the archangel Gabriel, Allah's messenger

Mika'il [*Arb.*]: the Islamic name for the archangel Michael, leader of the army of Allah against the forces of evil

Azra'il or Izra'il [*Arb.*]: the Islamic name for the archangel Azrael, the Angel of Death

Israfil [*Arb.*]: the fourth of the Islamic archangels; Israfil will blow the trumpet from a holy rock in Jerusalem to announce the Day of Resurrection

chempaka [*b.m.*]: the chempaka tree or Magnolia champaca is a large evergreen tree, native to Southeast Asia, known for its fragrant yellow or white flowers

address to Allah: the dawn or Fajr prayers, the first of the five Muslim obligatory prayers

Pa-Chi or **Pakcik** [*b.m.*]: uncle; a term of deference to address an older man regardless of kinship.

Two Faces

caladium: a flowering plant with large, arrowhead-shaped leaves marked in varying patterns in either white, pink or red

Pangolin

Kuching: capital of Sarawak, located on the northern coast of Malaysia; Nalpon was a disc jockey and journalist based for some time in Sarawak around 1960
museum: Sarawak State Museum, Kuching

The Appointment

Dacron: a synthetic polyester fabric.
Nikki [*aut.*]: Nalpon gave his wife a similar donkey that wore tight chequered trousers; it was called Mikki instead of Nikki
Leucona's Andalucía: a composition by Cuban composer Ernesto Lecuona (1895-1963); the popular song "The Breeze and I" (1941) is based on the Andalucía suite and its lyrics appear to have inspired this story
Ruggiero Ricci: American violinist (1918-2012) renowned for his recordings of the works of Paganini
cathedral bells [*aut.*]: almost certainly emanating from Singapore's Catholic cathedral, the Cathedral of the Good Shepherd in Queen Street, close to SJI's original site on Bras Basah Road; Nalpon married his wife Mona here in 1962

The Grasshopper Trappers

morbok [*b.m.*] or merbok: zebra dove, popular as pets because of their tuneful song

The One-Eyed Widow of Bukit Ho Swee

Bukit Ho Swee: in the west of Singapore, closest to the existing Tiong Bahru estate; well-known because of its tragic historical past—in the Bukit Ho Swee fire of 25 May 1961, four people died, eighty-five were injured and 16,000 people were made homeless
Singapore Improvement Trust (SIT): set up by the colonial British government in 1927 to tackle the problem of housing in Singapore; in 1960, the SIT was replaced by the Housing Development Board (HDB)

The Hunter Lays Down His Spear

Employment Act: "Enacted in 1968 to provide for the basic terms and working conditions for all types of employees except those employed in managerial or executive positions, seamen and domestic workers" (http://www.mom.gov.sg/legislation/Pages/labour-relations.aspx, accessed 14 February 2013)

Ministry of Labour: either of the postwar Ministries (Ministry of Labour and Social Welfare and later the Ministry of Labour and Law) preceding the current Ministry of Manpower, which was established c. 1998

The Mango Tree

hammered seven [...] confined the spirit dog: Malay superstition; using nails to prevent ghosts from descending from trees is a traditional practice

The Courtship of Donatello Varga

A longer manuscript version of Nalpon's "A Girl as Sweet as Alice", a story published posthumously in Robert Yeo, ed., *Singular Stories* (1993)

Fabian: Fabiano Anthony Forte (b. 6 February 6 1943), an American singer, actor and teen idol of the late 1950s and early 1960s

Gerry Mulligan: Gerald Joseph 'Gerry' Mulligan (6 April 1927–20 January 1996), an American jazz saxophonist, clarinettist, composer and arranger, but not a trombone player

Casanova: Giacomo Girolamo Casanova de Seingalt (1725–1798), Italian adventurer; a name now synonymous with 'womaniser'

his missing front teeth [*aut.*]: Nalpon himself had all his teeth removed in early adulthood

Brigitte Bardot: Brigitte Anne-Marie Bardot (b. 1934), French actress, singer and fashion model; well-known sex symbol of the 1950s and 1960s

Robinson Road: major road in the centre of Singapore city; c. 1960 still a seaside thoroughfare

A Man Without Song

The title of this story and first two sentences derive from a passage in *Cup of Gold* (1929) the first novel by John Steinbeck (one of Nalpon's favourite writers). Merlin tells a Welsh peasant: "I have grown to be a man [...] and there be no songs in a man. Only children make songs—children and idiots."

bee hoon factory [*aut.*]: there was a bee hoon factory (as well as a Buddhist temple) neighbouring the Nalpon family's old house at Jalan Soo Bee, Changi

(Jacinta Nalpon, conversation, September 2011).

kati [*b.m.*]: a traditional Malay common unit of measurement of mass; approximately 1.5 pounds or 0.7 kilogrammes

1938 [*aut.*]: the year that Nalpon was born

1.6 kilometres (a mile): Singapore had recently discarded the colonial British mile for kilometres as a measure of distance

liver […] and brandy: almost certainly a reference to confinement food; after giving birth, Chinese women are traditionally 'confined' for a month (hence the shuttered room) and consume nourishing food such as liver (to replenish blood loss), brandy (for strength) and tonics; some confinement dishes are made with sesame oil

her stomach was bound: binding the stomach is a Malay tradition

Kempetai: Japanese military police corps roughly equivalent to Nazi Germany's Gestapo

National Productivity board (NPB): established in 1972 to improve productivity in all sectors of Singapore's economy

Liberation Day: Singapore was officially returned to British colonial rule on 12 September 1945

general strike: there was a two day general strike in January 1946, organised by the Malayan Communist Party

Lion City Filled With Panthers

In March 1973, a panther escaped from Mandai Zoo; in July 1975, the 'Tanjong Rhu panther' was captured.

The pattern of the panther can be destroyed!: the article ends with the editorial note: "Gregory Nalpon is a former trade unionist"; this, coupled with the reference to the Tanjong Rhu panther, suggests the date of this article as shortly after July 1975

Radin

ponkis [*b.m.*]: a kind of rattan bakul or basket usually filled with stones and bait deployed on the seabed to catch crabs

The Open Air Market

Murillo: Bartolomé Esteban Murillo (1617–82), Spanish Baroque painter, known for religious works and lively, realist paintings of contemporary women and children

Mei-Lin [b]

kelong [*b.m.*]: "A large fish trap built with stakes, common along the coasts of the Malay Peninsula; also, a building erected over one" (OED)

black mollies: South American freshwater fish sold to be kept in aquariums; the males are mildly aggressive

swordtails: another popular aquarium fish

Shaw Brothers: film studio owned by Shaw Brothers (HK) Ltd, the foremost, largest movie production company of Hong Kong movies; renowned during the 1960s and 1970s for their martial arts movies.

Ipoh: capital city of Perak state, North Malaysia

Orpheus: musician, poet, and prophet in ancient Greek religion and myth, who could charm all living things and even stones with his music; Orpheus attempted to save his wife, Eurydice, from the underworld

The Moment of Truth

Hang Tuah: legendary Malay warrior of the fifteenth century

My Say

Degas: Edgar Degas (1834–1917), French impressionist painter and sculptor, especially identified with the subject of dance

El Salón México: a symphonic composition (1936) in one movement by American classical composer Aaron Copland (1900–90), which makes extensive use of Mexican folk music

Well Jacinta […] wisely [*aut.*]: this passage is an excerpt from a letter Nalpon wrote for his daughter on her first birthday; he wrote another for her thirteenth birthday in 1976

The Wayang at Eight Milestone

There was an 'Eight Milestone' (i.e. indicating eight miles from the Singapore city centre) at Seletar Road, Changi Road and Bukit Timah; a cemetery near the Eight Milestone at Bukit Timah indeed existed, and is the probable location for this story

Changi bus terminus: at Eight Milestone on Changi Road, near the original site of the Anglican High School

wayang [*b.m.*]: a theatrical outdoor performance employing puppets (Indonesian) or human actors in elaborate costumes and make-up; in Singapore, the reference is now almost exclusive to Chinese opera

Author Timeline

DATES	NALPON'S LIFE	SOCIO-HISTORICAL-LITERARY CONTEXT
6 February 1938	Birth, Jalan Soo Bee, Changi	
1939		Singapore completes the main British naval base, which is the largest drydock and third largest floating dock in the world
1942-5		Japanese invasion and occupation of Singapore
1947		A large number of strikes occur, causing stoppages in public transport, public services and harbour work
1948-60		Malayan 'Emergency'
1949-1954	Attends Saint Joseph's Institution, Bras Basah Road; friends and classmates include Patrick Zehnder and Patrick Mowe	1950: Maria Hertogh riots 1954: Founding of People's Action Party
1954		Chinese school students demonstrate against the British due to the National Service proposal
1955		Four people are killed during the Hock Lee bus riots
1957	Presents music review programme *Music Shop Review* at 8pm on Radio Singapore	Malaya achieves independence

October 1957	With Derek Cooper, presents *Radio Gazette* on Radio Singapore, 9pm	
Late 1950s	Travels in Thailand, Malaysia and Sarawak	
1959		First government of State of Singapore; Lee Kuan Yew, Prime Minister
1960	Branch union official for Singapore Manual Mercantile Workers Union (SMMWU)	Housing Development Board replaces Singapore Improvement Trust
1961	Writes and presents series of short radio broadcasts, *Window on Asia*	Many legislators leave PAP to join Barisan Socials (Socialist Front); Bukit Ho Swee Fire kills four people and destroys 2,200 attap houses
1962	Sent to Australia and Russia on radio journalism assignments by Rediffusion; marries Mona Soliano, at Cathedral of the Good Shepherd, Queen Street	
1963	Birth of daughter, Jacinta	Formation of Malaysia, including Singapore; during Operation Coldstore, 107 left-wing politicians and trade unionists are arrested by Internal Security Department
1964	Birth of son, Zero; leaves Rediffusion.	Riots in July and September involving Malays and Chinese
1965		9 August: Singapore ejected from Malaysia, becomes independent nation
1965-75	Union advocate; appears in Singapore's courts as union representative for aggrieved members	

25 June 1966	In Singapore's second arbitration court, Nalpon accuses the management of a local shipping company of trying to "smash the union" after 43 employees were sacked without due cause	
1967		The first batch of the army is drafted for national service
1968		PAP wins all seats in the General Election, which is boycotted by Barisan Sosialis
1969	June: attempts to defend workers' pension rights against major local engineering firm, accuses employer of "abusing labour laws"; loses case defending 28 employees' jobs at local ad agency	May: Riots in Singapore and Malaysia, involving Malays and Chinese
December 1970	Wins case and ensures payment of bonuses and medical benefits for 150 employees of piling firm	PAP suppresses local tea dances and samshu shops
1971	Wins case at Arbitration Court, forcing leading furniture firm to discuss new 'incentive plan' with union representatives	October: Last British military forces withdraw from Singapore
1972		PAP wins the General Election
29 November 1974	Dramatically produces $60 SGD wastepaper basket at Industrial Arbitration court, as an example of local international school's lavish spending while refusing to pay salaries recommended by National Wages Council to 170 local employees	

1975	Ceases work with union, begins to focus on writing	
1974-5	Series of stories and an essay appear in *Her World*	
3 August 1975	"A Man Without Song" published in *The Straits Times*	
1976		PAP wins all 69 seats in the General Election
1976-7	Employed by SeaAir	
1977	Employed by Reuters	
1977-8	Part-time journalism	
1978	"The Rose and the Silver Key" included in *Singapore Short Stories*, ed. by Robert Yeo	
28 September 1978	Dies suddenly from heart attack	
1979		Speak Mandarin Campaign inaugurated by Lee Kuan Yew
23-28 July 1991	Dramatised version of "The Rose and the Silver Key" adapted by Stella Kon, performed by Act 3 Theatre Company before thousands of secondary school students in Singapore at the old Drama Centre, Fort Canning	
1991-2	Robert Yeo's *Singapore Short Stories* featuring "The Rose and the Silver Key", becomes the second local text to be included as a GCE O-Level Literature in English text	

1992	Norman Ware and Robert Yeo attempt to publish a collection of Nalpon's stories; the project is abandoned as Ware and Yeo can only trace six stories
1993	"A Girl as Sweet as Alice" [an edited version of "The Courtship of Donatello Varga"] appears in *Singular Stories*, ed. by Robert Yeo

About the Author

Gregory Nalpon was born in 1938 in Singapore. After attending St Joseph's Institution, he energetically embarked on a variety of peripatetic careers: disc jockey, journalist, trade unionist and 'gentleman of leisure'. These assorted vocations took him from Singapore to Sarawak, Northern Malaysia, Thailand and Australia. During the 1960s and 1970s, Nalpon composed numerous stories, essays, plays and novels. His short story, "The Rose and the Silver Key" was studied by thousands of Singaporean secondary school students. With Nalpon's sudden death in 1978 at the age of 40, the majority of his writings remained unpublished for over thirty years.

About the Editor

Angus Whitehead is an Assistant Professor at the National Institute of Education, Nanyang Technological University, Singapore. He has published a number of papers, reviews and interviews related to literature in Singapore, and is currently editing a collection of short fiction by acclaimed poet Arthur Yap. A William Blake specialist, he is co-editor of a collection of essays, *Re-envisioning Blake* (2012). Currently based in the west of Singapore, Angus remains committed to recovering and exploring other roads less travelled in Singaporean literary history.